THE
HIDDEN
QUARRY

Also by Ron Base

Fiction
Matinee Idol
Foreign Object
Splendido
Magic Man
The Strange
The Sanibel Sunset Detective
The Sanibel Sunset Detective Returns
Another Sanibel Sunset Detective
The Two Sanibel Sunset Detectives
The Hound of the Sanibel Sunset Detective
The Confidence Man
The Four Wives of the Sanibel Sunset Detective
The Escarpment
The Sanibel Sunset Detective Goes to London
Heart of the Sanibel Sunset Detective
The Dame with the Sanibel Sunset Detective
The Mill Pond
I, The Sanibel Sunset Detective
Main Street, Milton
Bring Me the Head of the Sanibel Sunset Detective

Dark Edge Novellas
The White Island
The Secret Stones

Non-fiction
The Movies of the Eighties (with David Haslam)
If the Other Guy Isn't Jack Nicholson, I've Got the Part
Marquee Guide to Movies on Video
Cuba Portrait of an Island (with Donald Nausbaum)

www.ronbase.com
Contact Ron at
ronbase@ronbase.com

RON BASE

THE HIDDEN QUARRY

A NOVEL OF SUSPENSE

West-End
Books

Library and Archives Canada Cataloguing in Publication
Title: The hidden quarry / Ron Base.
Names: Base, Ron, author.
Description: Series statement: The Milton mysteries; 4
Identifiers: Canadiana 20200237063 | ISBN 9780994064592 (softcover)
Classification: LCC PS8553.A784 H54 2020 | DDC C813/.54—dc23

West-End Books
133 Mill St.
Milton, Ontario
L9T 1S1

Text design and electronic formatting: Ric Base
Cover design and coordination: Jennifer Smith
Author photo: Katherine Lenhoff

"Listen to me," cried Syme with extraordinary emphasis. "Shall I tell you the secret of the whole world? It is that we have only known the back of the world. We see everything from behind, and it looks brutal. That is not a tree, but the back of a tree. That is not a cloud, but the back of a cloud. Cannot you see that everything is stooping and hiding a face? If we could only get round in front."

— **G.K. Chesterton**

Readers should know there is a real place called Milton. From Toronto, you drive west an hour or so (depending on traffic), turn south on Highway 25, and soon you have reached the town. That's the real Milton. The Milton you will read about in the following pages, while accurate insofar as setting, is, nonetheless, a fictional Milton, the Milton out of this author's slightly diabolical imagination.

1

The two bodies were like ivory shards on the emerald water of the Hidden Quarry.

The quarry had been abandoned years ago, exhausted of its limestone, sand and gravel, the aggregate that once fed road and building construction across the Greater Toronto Area. Left were great chunks of battlement-like rock formations descending into an open pit fifty feet deep and filled with alkaline water.

And the bodies.

Two hikers, a young man and woman, had stopped on a rocky outcropping above the pond, admiring it before embracing and kissing. "We're right out in the open," the woman murmured against his mouth.

"No one around for miles," the man said.

They kissed some more. The woman allowed the man to unbutton her blouse. The man unhooked her bra so he could turn her around, her back against him, and caress her breasts. In broad daylight, she thought vaguely, out in the open, and she was allowing it.

Enjoying it. The new freedom, she thought.

It was while he was fondling her that she noticed something in the water below.

The woman moved away to peer down, trying to get a closer look, not sure what she was seeing with the sunlight speckling the water.

"What's wrong?" asked the man.

"There's something down there," the woman said. She shrugged back into her blouse, disappointing her companion.

"I can't see anything," he said, bending to retrieve the discarded brassiere.

"We should take a look," the woman said.

"Stay put," the man said. "I'll check it out."

He made his way down through thick forest surrounding the pit, breaking onto a narrow shoreline, the massiveness of the cliff walls jutting up around him on three sides.

"Those are bodies," the woman called down, fear edging her voice.

The man used his hand to shade his eyes. "Jesus," he breathed, realizing the two forms in the water were in fact bodies.

He groped for the cellphone in the side pocket of his shorts. He dialed 911.

Above, on the cliff, the woman was trying to control her panic, her mind swirling with the possible disastrous outcomes from being at this quarry with this man and those bodies. She should not be here. It was careless of her to have had anything to do with this guy, let alone end up in bed with him and then, in a moment of unthinking weakness, agree to go hiking with him. What was she thinking?

Her husband would kill her.

She began to have difficulty breathing. Down on the shore, she could see the man on his cell phone. Then he called up to her. She couldn't hear what he was saying. It didn't make any difference. She couldn't be here.

She turned and bolted away.

2

Jean Whitlock loved Otis, her German Shepherd dog, and hated her garden.

In about equal measure.

Everything was green. Nothing seemed to be flowering. Mind you, the summer had come late to Milton after a particularly brutal winter. Everything was slow coming in, this according to gardeners who knew of these things.

Jean knew nothing.

She had bought the small one-story house on James Street with an impressive garden and neighbors who spent a great deal of time and effort making sure their gardens looked spectacular. Jean, therefore, was embarrassed into doing something she had no interest in doing.

Gardening.

Which was probably why everything looked kind of dead. Why nothing was flowering.

Damn!

Sensing her frustration, Otis heaved himself up from the patch of grass where he had been sunning himself and trotted over. She hugged him against her. He made pleased sounds.

"You're the dog I shouldn't have, Otis," she said to him, "along with the garden I shouldn't be allowed in. The difference is, against all my better instincts, I have fallen in love with you. Meanwhile, I hate—*hate*—this garden."

Otis stretched out beside her. She was no good at this, she thought. No good at gardening. No good at domesticity. Doing the things everyone expected of you when you owned a house. She shouldn't be allowed to own a house. She shouldn't be allowed in a garden. She shouldn't be back in the small town where she grew up and where as a kid she had wanted to do nothing more than get out.

When it came right down to it, she thought, tearing off her work gloves in frustration, she was no good at life. Period.

At least not *this* life.

In her other life, her former life as a corporal with the Royal Canadian Mounted Police, she was a pretty darned good police officer. That was her life for many years, the life where you didn't have to worry about gardens or dogs or being domestic. All you had to worry about was bringing the bad guys to justice. Compared to making a garden grow, the bad guys were easy.

From inside the house she heard the phone start to ring. Otis raised his head expectantly. Whoever was calling at least saved her from further rumination and recrimination—for the time being. She hurried inside and grabbed the phone.

"Jean," a gravelly voice pronounced as soon as she picked up the receiver.

Jean groaned inwardly. "Aunt Alice," she said aloud.

"It's been a while," Alice Whitlock said. "We haven't had a chance to talk since you got back."

"No," Jean said, thinking, whose fault is that?

"I was in Europe and unfortunately had to miss your mother's funeral. Did you get my card?"

"Very kind," Jean said, not sure if she got any card from Alice.

"And of course, your brother's death and then Mayor Jock, so sad, so much tragedy and scandal. How are you doing?"

"I'm fine, Alice," Jean said. "It's kind of you to ask."

"You've had a time of it, that's for sure," Alice said. "I understand you're staying on in Milton."

"For the time being," Jean said.

"You've bought a house, I understand."

"Yes."

"Well, that sounds like more than just 'for the time being.'"

"I've got the house, it's the rest of it I'm not so sure about."

"I see," Alice said. "Well, the reason I'm calling today, Jean…"

"Yes?"

"There is a situation that's come up you may be able to help with," Alice said, pleasantries over; time to get down to business.

"What kind of situation?"

"My late husband's niece," Alice said. "I don't think you ever met Daye."

"Daye Whitlock?"

"She's Daye Parker now."

"I didn't know Daye married."

"Married and separated," Alice said. "Honestly, that child. You ask me, she's always been wild. She never should have dropped out of school. She should have pursued a career, but she could never settle down. If she had listened to me, she wouldn't have married this character in the first place. But she wouldn't listen and now she's in the fix that she's in."

Jean knew she was going to regret it but nonetheless she asked, "What kind of 'fix' is she in, Alice?"

"What other kind of fix is there for a young woman like her? The kind of fix only a man can get you in."

"Tell me what's going on."

"He's making her life totally miserable, that's what's going on," Alice stated firmly. "He's beaten her, threatened her, and he follows her everywhere. Her life has become a living hell, let me tell you."

"Who, Alice? Who's doing this to her?"

Alice sounded exasperated. "Her husband, of course. Who else would it be?"

"The husband being?"

"Doyle Parker, for heaven's sake." Alice stated this in a way that suggested Jean should already have that information. "As unpleasant an individual as ever breathed air," she added.

"Are they still together?" Jean asked.

"Are you kidding?" Alice sounded disdainful. "They are *supposed* to be separated. He is *supposed* to leave her alone. She is *supposed* to be getting on with her life. She is *supposed* to be doing all those things, but instead she's living under constant threat. As it is, she's afraid to leave the house."

"Has she gone to the police?"

"The police." Alice sounded even more disdainful. "The police have done nothing. There's a restraining order but all that's done is make the situation worse for her."

"Even so," Jean said, "in a situation like this, they're probably Daye's best bet."

"No, they're not," Alice said decisively. "That's why I'm calling you, Jean. You are a former Royal Canadian Mounted Police officer. You have experience with situations like this."

"Like you said, Alice. I'm a *former* officer. I've got no authority to do anything."

"You can do something to stop this man," Alice said in a strained voice. "Otherwise, I swear he's going to kill her." Alice's voice broke. "That's where this is going to end if he isn't stopped. Daye's going to end up murdered by this terrible, awful man."

Jean would like to have said something reassuring, an argument that might temper Alice's mounting hysteria. But she knew the statistics when it came to domestic violence. If Daye's estranged husband was threatening her, then in all likelihood the threat was serious. Doyle Parker, given his actions, might very well kill his wife.

Alice said, "Daye's up in Georgetown, scared out of her mind. I'd like you to go up there and see what you can do to stop this."

An impossible request, Jean immediately thought. But she didn't say that to Alice. Instead, she asked, "Does Daye know you're talking to me?"

"No, no," Alice said quickly. "She'd have a fit if she knew I called you. She doesn't want to be a bother to anyone. She finds this whole thing embarrassing. But like I said, I'm afraid something terrible is going to happen. I'd never forgive myself if I stayed silent."

"Look, why don't I drive up there and see if she's all right," Jean said. "If there's something I can do to help, I'll be happy to do it."

Alice's voice flooded with relief. "You have no idea how much I appreciate this, Jean."

"Her husband is Doyle Parker."

"That's right."

"Do you know what he does for a living?"

"He works in a quarry up there. What's it called? A really stupid name for a quarry if you ask me. Halton Rock Quarry. That's it."

"What about Daye? Is she working?"

"She worked as a receptionist for some insurance company in town, but I don't think she's there any longer."

"Give me her address," Jean said.

3

"They're two young women of what appears to be Asian origin, in their twenties," said Irwin "Doc" Prescott, the district medical examiner.

"Any idea what happened to them, Doc?" asked Halton Detective Mickey Dann. He stood beside his partner, Glen Petrusiak, the men huddled along the narrow shoreline sloping down from the woods. The corpses of the two women lay nearby beneath white shrouds.

"No idea right now," Doc said. "There are contusions on their faces and arms. Hard to say what caused them. If they drowned, their lungs will be full of water. But I won't know that until I get them back to the morgue. The contusions could mean something other than accidental death. We'll see."

"Two young women found in an abandoned quarry where no one goes swimming. Come on, Doc, this has gotta be a homicide," Glen Petrusiak said.

Doc blessed Petrusiak with a doleful eye. "I forget what a forensics expert our former Toronto detective is."

"We've got officers searching the area, but so far no one's found clothes that should belong to the victims," Mickey interjected. "No sign of an abandoned vehicle back on the road, either."

Doc Prescott shrugged. "Even though it's our friend here, and I never like to agree with him, in this case he might be right. It certainly looks suspicious."

One of the crime scene investigators, a ghostly figure in a white Tyvek protective suit contrasting to the greenery of the encroaching woods, took photographs. Another investigator walked the scene with a video camera. In the woods beyond, Mickey could see officers continuing their search for evidence that might help identify the women. So far, they had found nothing.

Mickey turned to Petrusiak. "Where's the guy who discovered the bodies?"

"Back at the roadway. His name's Curtis King. He's crabbing because we won't let him go."

"You stay here and continue to give Doc Prescott a bad time," Mickey said. He started off and then stopped. "Let's get the OPP in here with their divers and have them search the water in the quarry."

"You're kidding," Petrusiak said.

"No clothes, no vehicle, and two nude bodies. How did they get here?"

"Someone dumped them," Petrusiak countered.

"Could be," Mickey said agreeably. "But then maybe not. Order up the divers."

"I'm going to have to get authorization," Petrusiak said. "I'm not so sure I'm going to get it."

"Let's try," Mickey said.

Mickey climbed the steep hillside to the gravel roadway above the quarry where dozens of police and emergency vehicles were lined up. Nearby, a female officer watched over a Ford Expedition with its liftback up. Constable Dara Tate was small and dark and interesting, much too interesting, Mickey thought as he nodded at her. The least interesting thing about her was that she had recently become engaged to Glen Petrusiak. She waved at him, he slowed so that she could come over.

"There's a backpack in the rear of his vehicle." She spoke in a low voice.

"Is that so?" answered Mickey noncommittally.

"I probably shouldn't have, but I took a peek inside."

"Okay," Mickey said.

"There's a woman's bra in there," the officer said.

Mickey took this in. "Thanks," he said.

She lowered her voice more. "Am I going to see you later?"

Shit, he thought.

Curtis King leaned against one of the police cruisers, his arms folded, looking impatient as Mickey approached. "Mr. King, I'm Detective Mickey Dann."

King reluctantly took the detective's offered hand. "Are you the guy who can get me out of here?"

"A couple of questions and then you can go."

King looked irritated. He was short and wiry, Nike shorts and top on a runner's body. "I've been answering questions for the last three hours. I don't know what else I can say. I was hiking out here. I'd heard about this abandoned quarry, the Hidden Quarry as everyone around here calls it. Supposed to be pretty spectacular. But I wasn't quite sure where it was. When I found it, I noticed something in the water. I got closer and saw the two bodies. I called 911. Not a whole lot more complicated than that."

"You were hiking alone?"

"Yes," he said.

"You're sure about that?"

"Of course, I'm sure." King was more agitated, arms tightly folded, stiffening against the car. "Why wouldn't I be sure?"

"If I told you Mr. King that you were with a woman when you discovered the bodies, what would you say?"

"I would say that's not the case," King answered.

"All right, then," Mickey said. "I appreciate your cooperation."

"Does that mean I can go now?"

"Of course," Mickey said. "And thanks again."

Curtis King dropped his arms, straightening from the car. "This has been pretty traumatic."

"I imagine it has," Mickey said.

"Any idea what happened to those women?"

"Not yet. The investigation is in the early stages."

"I don't know where you got the idea I was with someone," King said.

"If there's anything else you want to tell us…" Mickey allowed his voice to trail off.

"No, I've told you everything."

Mickey handed him a card. "That's my cell. If you think of anything else or if there is something you decide you want to tell me, please call."

King held the card. "I've got to get home to my wife," he said. "She'll be wondering what's happened."

Mickey watched him as he walked back toward his vehicle. He watched Dara Tate move away from his vehicle. She smiled at King. Nice smile, Mickey thought. King looked momentarily beguiled. Dara could have that effect on you, Mickey decided.

As King drove away, Petrusiak reached the roadway, looking winded. He went to Dara and spoke to her. She used that beguiling smile again. Petrusiak melted. Then he walked to Mickey, looking too self-satisfied for there to be anything but news that served Petrusiak's interests.

Sure enough.

"Chief say no divers."

"You phoned the chief?"

"Like I said, I thought I'd better check with him," Petrusiak said. "He says it looks like an accidental drowning. We're wasting our time out here, let alone wasting money on divers."

"The chief says that, does he?"

"I agree with him if you want to know," Petrusiak said.

"A moment ago, you were telling the medical examiner it was a homicide."

"Was I?" Petrusiak smiled, and walked off.

Bastard, Mickey thought. He looked down the road at Dara. She saw him and smiled.

That smile.

4

Jean drove north on Sixth Line. Doyle Parker didn't show up on social media but there was a photograph of him embracing Daye on her Facebook page. A big strapping guy, by the look of him. In the photo he wore a tight white T-shirt showing off rippling biceps and a right arm filled with swirling tattoos. If she had to read the expression on a handsome face marked by a two-day beard growth, she would say it was one of smug complacency, a man certain of his special place in his small world.

In short, an asshole.

Or maybe, she thought ruefully as she turned onto Trafalgar Road, she was reading too much into a single photograph.

Or, given the circumstances, maybe not.

A paved road flanked by artfully arranged boulders marked the turnoff for the Halton Rock Quarry. Jean thought of turning in but lacking a ready explanation why she might be there, she parked across the road.

And waited.

For the next hour or so a line of big trucks moved in and out of the quarry, throwing up clouds of dust so that when Doyle Parker appeared behind the wheel of a dirt-streaked Dodge Ram, she almost missed him. But no, that was him, having to slow for the two trucks ahead, impatiently hitting his horn. Assholes, Jean had long since decided, drove trucks, wore baseball caps, and used their horns at the slightest provocation.

Doyle even wore a baseball cap, the brim pulled down to shade his eyes.

Once he freed himself from the slow-moving trucks, Doyle gunned it and, adding to Jean's view of his asshole status, sped into Georgetown. He slowed a bit coming along Maple Avenue onto Main Street South, divided by a flower-choked median. He turned right on Mill Street and parked in front of a white wood-frame bungalow fronted by a white porch adorned with hanging flower pots filled with petunias. Jean pulled her vehicle over and parked a hundred yards or so behind Doyle's Dodge.

She watched as he got out and strode up the porch steps, tried the screen door, found it locked and then began to pound on it. The echo of his blows reverberated along the street. Finally, the door opened, allowing Doyle to charge inside.

Jean reached under her seat where she kept her retractable police baton and then got out of the car.

She walked swiftly along the street to the white-frame house. The screen door was ajar. She went up the steps, hearing angry shouts from the inside. Jean pushed the door open and stepped into a hallway. She could hear a man's voice yelling, "Who the hell is it? You bitch!"

"There's no one!" Daye's voice—a desperate cry.

"Bullshit! Who is it?"

Jean marched down the hall into a kitchen where a young woman in jeans and a white blouse sat cowering at a table. Doyle Parker was tensed over her, the veins standing out on his muscular raised arm.

Jean called out, "Hey, there, cousin."

Doyle jerked around, his eyes widening in alarm. "What the hell?" he said.

Daye Parker turned a tear-stained face to Jean, her eyes filling with a combination of fear and relief.

"I hope I haven't come at a bad time," Jean added.

Doyle's face had lost its surprise, darkening into a sullenness framed with anger. "Who are you?" he demanded.

Jean ignored him, focusing on Daye. "I was in the neighborhood. Aunt Alice suggested I drop around and say hello."

"Get out of here," Doyle snapped.

Jean allowed her gaze to drift in Doyle's direction. "I'm sorry, I should have introduced myself. I'm Daye's cousin, Jean Whitlock. I didn't catch your name."

"I'm her goddamn husband is who I am and I want you out of here."

"I guess that would make you Doyle Parker." Jean looked at Daye. "What about it, Daye? Do you want me out?"

Daye looked confused. "I—I don't want any trouble," she said in a quiet, scared voice.

"I know you don't," Jean said. She returned her gaze to Doyle. "You know, I got the impression when I came in that you were just about to hit my cousin. Am I right about that, Doyle?"

His face had darkened even more. "Get out!" he yelled.

"Answer the question. Were you just about to hit your wife? Because if you were, that wouldn't be right and I wouldn't like it."

Doyle's charge at Jean was drawn to an abrupt stop when she snapped the baton out to its full length. "I wouldn't like that at all," she added.

Doyle, frozen in place, showed a combination of anger and uncertainty.

Jean said, "I'd appreciate it if I could visit with Daye for a while. I understand you're not supposed to be here. There's a restraining order that prevents you from entering the house. Is that right, Doyle?"

"It's my goddamn house," he said.

"Tell you what. You leave right now and that way you don't get into trouble and I can chat with Daye."

Doyle's eyes narrowed as though trying to gauge what he was up against with this woman who unexpectedly confronted him. "Who are you?" he demanded finally.

"Someone you don't want any trouble with," Jean answered.

"You think I'm afraid of a woman?" he sneered.

"I think you're smart enough to know you don't want trouble with me."

Doyle took a deep breath and turned to Daye. "I'll talk to you later."

Daye looked up at him with desperate eyes. He touched her shoulder. She flinched. Jean tensed.

Doyle smirked as he brushed past Jean and went out the door.

When he was gone, Daye breathed a palpable sigh of relief. Then she began to cry. Jean saw a box of tissues on the kitchen counter, retrieved a couple and handed them to Daye.

"It's all right," Jean said.

"No, it isn't," Daye said, using one of the tissues to dry her eyes. "You shouldn't have done that."

"I wasn't going to stand there while he beat you up."

"I'm not even sure who you are." Daye used another tissue on her eyes.

"Our Aunt Alice called and said you were in trouble. It looks like you are."

"He'll just come back," she said in a resigned voice. "There's no getting rid of him."

"Maybe I can help," Jean offered.

Daye rewarded her with an impatient look. "Yeah? How are you going to do that?"

"For one thing, we could talk to the Halton Police."

"The police won't do anything, they're useless."

"I'm a former police officer."

"I've heard about you," Daye said in a unfriendly voice. "You were kicked out of the Mounties."

"More to the point, I know the police in Halton," Jean said. "Let me talk to them for you."

"I don't want the police, okay?" Daye snapped.

"Sure, if that's how you feeling," Jean said.

"Look, I'm sorry, I really am." Daye got to her feet. "I appreciate what you did, don't get me wrong. But I'm not feeling so well. I'd rather be left alone right now."

"Let me at least give you my phone number," Jean said. There was a note pad and pen on the counter. "If you think you're in danger or you just want to talk."

When she finished writing, she placed the notepad on the kitchen table. "Call it any time. Okay?"

Daye nodded without looking at the paper. "Yeah, sure," she said. "Whatever."

5

Doyle drove like a crazy man along unpaved roads, trying to relieve the pressure building inside him.

There were few cops on these back roads so he could get away with just about anything, go as fast as the Dodge Ram would allow, fishtailing all over the goddamn place, practically running off the road, thinking about killing himself and then deciding he wasn't going to give that bitch the satisfaction.

If he was going to kill anyone it should be her. Daye should be dead, not him. Her and that other bitch who showed up. Kind of a scary bitch, if he was being honest. Certain people, Doyle had discovered, allowed you to kick them around, no problem. His wife was a case in point. There were certain others you instinctively knew you had to be careful with.

That bitch was one of those people. What was her name, anyway? What'd she say, Jean? Was that it? He was in such a fury he hadn't paid the attention he should have paid.

Now he would pay attention, that was for damn sure. Wait a minute. His wife's maiden name. Whitlock. That was it.

Jean Whitlock.

Jean Whitlock would pay big time for dissing him in front of his wife. Kick her ass, the least of what he would do to her.

Doyle slowed as he passed the Halton Rock Quarry sign, accompanied by the announcement that there was NO TRESSPASSING. UNATHORIZED VISITORS WILL BE PROSECUTED.

Whatever that meant.

He drove past giant wheel loaders used to move dirt into massive rock trucks, and the crawler tractors that stripped away the rock. But the quarry was way past that at this stage of its life. Blasting was now required to extract what limestone and sandstone there was still available.

Doyle parked behind the double-wide office trailer that functioned as the headquarters of Halton Rock Quarry. He got out and went up the ramp leading to the entrance, steeling himself for the lion's den or, as he called it, the Shitbox.

The interior of the Shitbox certainly lived up to its nickname as far as Doyle was concerned: a jumble of metallic office desks, ancient filing cabinets and wall hangings featuring grimy photos of gravel pits. Dad Shirley, hump-backed, watery-eyed, his dusty trousers held up by suspenders, waved photographs at Doyle as he entered.

"New photos of the grandkids," Dad announced in his weak, husky voice. "Just arrived. Want to see 'em, Doyle?"

What was he supposed to say to that? "Sure," Doyle said.

Gail Shirley was seated at a desk at the back of the trailer, an immense fearsome woman with hair dyed a lustrous brown framing a deeply lined, deeply suspicious face obscured by the smoke from the cigarettes she fitted constantly into the corner of her thin line of a mouth. She said, "Dad, you're a fool where those kids are concerned."

Dad smiled, red-rimmed eyes sparkling as he displayed a couple of tow-haired little boys looking into the camera with what seemed to Doyle to be scared expressions. "Aren't they just the cutest damn things?"

Doyle peered at the photos Dad had stuck under his nose. "I thought they had dark hair."

"What do you mean?" Dad demanded.

"The last pictures you showed me, I thought the kids had dark hair."

"What the hell you talking about?" Dad, looking incensed, whipped the photos away. "You suggesting these aren't my grandkids?"

"Hey, they look different, that's all."

"They're not *different*," Dad said sullenly. "They're my grandkids."

Gail removed the cigarette from her mouth and blew a cloud of smoke before calling out: "Where the hell have you been, Doyle?"

"I had to speak to my wife," Doyle said.

Dad immediately looked more interested and less sullen. "How's that pretty lady doing, anyway?"

"Never better, Dad," Doyle answered. "I never felt so loved as I have with Daye. It's the real deal, let me tell you."

Gail was lighting another cigarette as she rose and came around the desk, moving slowly, like one of the earth movers down in the pit, Doyle thought. She gave him a stern look. "You haven't been beating on that woman again, have you, Doyle?"

Doyle looked offended. "I just said she's the love of my life."

"That's what you *say*. But what I *hear* is different from what you say."

"I don't know who would tell you different since there's nothing different to tell."

"Leave the boy alone, Gail," Dad interjected. "He's trying his best with that woman. Dealing with women in this day and age isn't easy for young fellas, that's for sure."

Gail gave him a fierce look. "You an expert in dealing with women, are you, Dad? Boy, you sure could have fooled me."

She returned her gaze to Doyle; a hard gaze, Doyle thought. What was it with all these tough, scary women, anyway? It was enough to make you wonder about a man's masculinity. Doyle dismissed the thought, then realized Gail was speaking to him.

"Sorry, ma'am. What's that you were saying?"

"Maybe you should stop beating the crap out of women and start listening to what I'm telling you."

"Yeah, sure. Sorry."

"I'm telling you to get your ass over to the compound, pick up the product and drive it into Toronto. The whales are calling."

Whales was the code word for the johns the girls serviced. When the whales called, that meant johns had placed orders for the girls or, as they were usually referred to, the product.

"I thought Karl was supposed to do that," Doyle said.

"You're working with Karl." Gail jabbed a finger into his chest. "You help him and quit bellyaching about it."

"Not bellyaching," Doyle protested.

"Then get out and do your job. Dad will give you the addresses."

"Don't be so hard on the lad." Dad was leaning on his cane, his breath coming in short explosions.

"Shut up, Dad," Gail snapped. "This son of a bitch gets himself arrested for domestic assault and who knows where that's gonna lead?"

"I'm not gonna get arrested," Doyle said.

"Tell that to your parole officer," Gail snapped.

"I already did," Doyle said.

She went back to her desk and lit another cigarette.

"Good god, woman." Dad raised that raspy voice of his. "You still got one burning."

Gail pointed her cigarette at Doyle. "You take those girls into town and that's it, Doyle. You don't touch them, understand?"

Doyle looked indignant. "I never touched any of those women."

"Yeah, and all men aren't assholes, and Dad doesn't have a cabin back there in the woods near the quarry where he occasionally avails himself of the product."

"That's an outrageous accusation," Dad blustered.

Gail jabbed her freshly lit cigarette at Doyle. "Get your ass in gear," she ordered.

The heat bubbled up inside him. He didn't need this shit, didn't need these goddamn women pushing him around. The white heat. It almost got the best of him. But then he took a deep breath and listened while Dad gave him the Toronto addresses for the whales.

One of these days, though, one of these days he would take care of Gail Shirley. He would take care of them all.

Jean Whitlock. That was her goddamn name.

One of these days.

6

By the time Doyle got to the compound where the Shirleys housed their women, the product was already in the Dodge Ram Pro Master cargo van.

Nataliya, a Ukrainian; Daria, from Latvia; Amber from—where? Some Midwestern U.S. city. Fergus Falls? Yeah that was it. Fergus goddamn Falls. Kiva was a tiny blonde from Estonia who said she was nineteen, and Bora, an almond-eyed twenty-year-old from South Korea.

And then there was Shanifa, Doyle's favorite, lean and dusky and dangerous-looking from some African backwater he could never remember. A high-cheek-boned beauty, Shanifa, cold and quiet and very desirable. Such flawlessly smooth chocolate skin. Full lips. Slightly upturned, darkly inquisitive eyes. He yearned to get his hands on her.

He tried to catch her eye as he got into the van. But she wasn't paying attention, head turned away, staring out the window, lost somewhere else, he concluded, far away from this place.

Daria and Nataliya were attractive enough, he supposed, but nothing like Shanifa. You could get pretty twisted up with a woman like Shanifa.

Karl, the big, nasty German clambered onboard. Small piggy eyes, and a thin wet mouth, blond hair shorn to a buzz cut, an Aryan prick as far as Doyle was concerned. Karl was the security guy for the Shirleys. He ensured that everyone was accounted for, going, and particularly coming back, no one over the allotted time unless the client was willing to pay. Karl looked after all that, not to mention applying the muscle where it was needed in order to keep everyone in line.

"Hey, Doyle," Karl called. "What are you waiting for? Let's get going."

What was he waiting for? Damnit, he had been waiting for Karl, the asshole. But Doyle didn't say anything. Best not to tangle with Karl, although the time would come, Doyle thought as he started up the van.

The time would come for everyone.

―――――――

When they got to Toronto, Nataliya was dropped off first, at an apartment complex in Forest Hill. Shanifa watched Karl escort her inside, taking note of the fact that Karl always stuck close; never letting his charges out of his sight until they were at the location agreed upon with the client. If an hour was agreed to, Karl was right back there on the dot to make the pickup. Karl was the dangerous one, she had concluded. There wasn't much she could do with him.

She noticed Doyle staring at her. Doyle was another matter entirely. She allowed him the hint of a smile. He liked that. Doyle liked her. Doyle she could do something with. If there was a weak link in this operation, Doyle was it.

"I know what you're thinking." Daria's voice was a whisper in her ear, breaking Shanifa's reverie.

Shanifa just looked at her.

"You're thinking there's a way out of this," Daria continued. "Well, there is not. Okay? You only get in trouble and when you are in trouble, we are all in trouble."

Shanifa didn't say anything. Instead, she concentrated on watching Karl as he returned to the van, noting his big, blubbery belly. He was strong, no question, but she wondered if he had any stamina. Perhaps not.

Daria gave Shanifa a cold stare as she left the van when it stopped in the Annex area of Toronto. This time Karl walked her to a Victorian-style townhouse with lovely gardens on either side of the entrance. This was the kind of house she would like to live in some day, Shanifa decided. It was going to take a while, though. First of all, she had to extricate herself from her present circumstance, not easy given women like Daria who didn't want to stir things up and therefore was probably an enemy rather than a friend.

When they arrived at their next location, Shanifa saw that the houses weren't houses at all. They were mansions, a tree-lined street full of mansions. She heard Doyle say something that sounded like "Rosedale." *Rosedale*, she repeated to herself, a name like heaven, a name that breathed the perfection of a fairyland. If you lived in a *Rosedale*, she decided, you could only be happy; there could not possibly be unhappy people in a land called *Rosedale*.

As Doyle came to a stop in front of a particularly impressive mansion at the end of a cul-de-sac, a cloud passed over her thoughts. If everything was perfect in Rosedale, then what was a woman like her doing here? If whoever dwelled in this grand house wanted her, then there must be darkness here as well as light.

She was about to enter the darkness.

7

Karl opened the front door into a paneled entrance hall. "Go in," he said gruffly. "The whale calls."

He closed the door, leaving Shanifa alone in this creepy place. There was an impressive staircase and to her right, an archway. From somewhere beyond that archway a voice called out, "I'm in here."

Shanifa entered a great room cast in shadow. At the far end, lit by a shaft of light from a nearby window, an elderly whale sat upon a throne-like chair. He sat with his legs crossed wearing an embroidered silk robe. Thick white hair was combed back from the sort of patrician face you would expect to find in a house like this. A dirty old man's face, Shanifa thought, free of any emotion. She worked up the smile required for the rich dirty old men who occupied her world.

"Come closer," the whale ordered in a hollow, disinterested voice.

When she approached, he nodded and said, "Yes." What was that? she wondered. Approval?

Apparently.

Rising to his feet, the whale let the robe drop open and she saw that he was naked. Her eyes focused on his distended white belly. He said, "I'm going upstairs to take a shower. I would like you to disrobe. Wait ten minutes and then come to the bedroom at the end of the hall. Do you understand that?"

Shanifa nodded.

"Ten minutes," the whale repeated.

He left the room. When she no longer could hear his footsteps, she breathed out and began to remove her clothes, laying them on a nearby sofa. When she was naked, she sat in the chair that the elderly man had just vacated.

And waited.

From somewhere upstairs, she thought she could hear the sound of a shower. Had ten minutes passed? She had no idea. Boredom, the anxiousness to get this over with, finally drove her to her feet.

She went into the hall and slowly climbed the stair-case. At the landing, the sound of the shower grew louder. The old whale was going to be very clean and smell good, she thought. That would make it easier, she told herself.

A strip of expensive-looking, ornately patterned carpet led to a bedroom at the end of the hall, its door ajar. She took her time following the carpet, thinking that the shower would stop soon and she would be with the whale.

She reached the door and pushed it open further, expecting to find the whale sprawled naked on the four-poster bed dominating the room. However, there was no sign of him and the bed did not look as though anyone had touched it.

The shower was still running. She gritted her teeth, hoping that this man did not want her to shower with him. She didn't want that. The idea repulsed her.

Instead of going into the bathroom, she perched on the edge of the bed, thinking that at any moment, he would turn off the shower and appear in the bedroom and they could get down to their business.

But the shower was not turned off and the old whale did not appear. Clouds of steam escaped out of the bathroom. That alarmed her. She got up from the bed and padded across thick wall-to-wall carpet. She paused, listening for a couple of minutes before pushing the bathroom door open wider and stepping inside.

Through a thick mist of steam, Shanifa could see through the glassed-in shower an assortment of carefully arranged showerheads spurting water full blast. She moved closer, trying to get a clearer view. She couldn't see the old whale. Her nose was practically pressed against the glass before she realized that he was on the floor, face down, blood running from his nose.

The blood swept away into the drain.

8

"I want you to handcuff me," Dara said.

Mickey said, "I'm not going to handcuff you, are you crazy?"

She giggled and poked at him. "You're so conservative."

"Does Glen handcuff you?"

"Glen." She made a face. "I've got to pee."

He watched her slip out of bed and into the bathroom, marveling once again at that small, compact irresistible body, the body that was capable of getting them both into a whole mess of trouble.

Dara left the bathroom door open as she squatted on the toilet. "What do you think?" she called.

He rolled onto his back and said, "What do I think about what?"

"About those bodies. Glen says it isn't homicide."

"Glen's sucking up to the chief."

She flushed the toilet and came back, diving into bed beside him. "Want to know what I think?"

"Sure, Constable," Mickey said. "Tell me what you think."

"I'm a woman, right?"

"You certainly are," Mickey agreed.

"There's no way I would end up at a quarry without any clothes unless someone dragged me there. I think someone murdered those two women and then dumped their bodies in that quarry."

"Make sure you tell Glen," Mickey said.

"I will, but in the meantime, you should get divers out to the quarry. There's something else there, I know it."

"The orders have come down from on high, no divers."

"I wouldn't listen to that," Dara said.

"You wouldn't, huh? What would you suggest?"

"I was reading about that former Mountie that you're in love with. Jean Whitlock?"

"I'm not in love with Jean," Mickey said.

"Yes, you are. You just won't admit it."

"You're crazy," Mickey said.

"I was reading about her, how the Mounties really screwed her over."

"You got that part right," Mickey said.

"She used to be a scuba diver. Did you know that?"

"No, as a matter of fact, I didn't."

"Get her to go in there. I'll bet you anything she'll find something."

"I'm already in enough trouble in this department," Mickey said.

"There wouldn't be any trouble if she found something."

"Let me think about it," Mickey said.

"I don't think you are thinking about that," Dara said. She took him in her hand. "You're thinking about something else."

"Yes," Mickey said.

―――――――

"How've you been?" Mickey asked when he got Jean on the line.

She kicked herself for allowing a feeling of surprise. She didn't want to be moved by him one way or the other; not expecting his calls and then being surprised when he did call.

"I've been just fine." Without you, she silently added, and then, "What about you?"

"Busy," Mickey replied, noncommittally. "Crime never sleeps."

"No kidding," Jean said, wondering where this was going.

"Let me ask you a question," Mickey said.

"Shoot," she said, wondering what she would say if he asked her out.

"I read somewhere that you were a certified scuba diver."

"I haven't dived in years, but yes," she answered, fighting to hide anything like a disappointed tone in her voice.

"I need your help," he said.

"Okay," Jean said carefully. "What is it you need?"

"A swim in a gravel pit," Mickey said.

Jean paused before she said, "Are you serious?"

"You probably read about the two women found floating in a quarry east of Georgetown."

"I don't read crime stories."

"We haven't been able to identify the women. They're young, Asian; we have our suspicions about what happened and who they are. But right now, it's a dead end. There's no sign of how the women ended up in the quarry. I think there might be something at the bottom, but my chief refuses to authorize a search. He thinks it's a waste of time and the department is stretched enough as it is."

"You want me to dive down and see if there's anything there?"

"Think of it as an opportunity for the two of us to get together," Mickey said. "It's overdue, don't you think?"

"Boy, you sure know how to charm a girl," Jean said.

"Will you do it?"

"When?"

"I'll pick you up this afternoon."

"That soon?"

"Maybe I can't wait to see you," Mickey said.

"Go to hell," she said.

"See you at two," he said.

Before she could respond, he hung up. She held the phone, swearing at it. Otis, stretched on the sofa she had told him many times not to lie on, cocked his head. "All men are assholes," Jean said to him. "Except you, of course, Otis."

9

Shanifa, after experimenting with various taps and handles was finally able to turn off the water.

She stared dispassionately at the body on the shower floor. The whale's eyes were wide open, staring at nothing, his mouth agape as though trying to speak words he would never speak again.

In her life, Shanifa had seen enough death to know he was dead. If he was still alive, fine, but she wasn't about to help him. One dead whale was one dead whale she didn't have to sleep with. Assuming he was dead, Shanifa also knew that, given her history, being found in this house would only place her in a great deal of jeopardy.

She left the bathroom and went downstairs and put her clothes back on. She took a deep breath, calming herself, trying to decide what to do. The old man had booked three hours. Time had passed. It wouldn't be long before Karl showed up to add to the trouble she was already in.

There was nothing in the living room that told her where she was or that revealed the identity of the man upstairs. She entered a kitchen so perfect it was as though no one had ever been in it, let alone cooked anything. How could you live in a place without leaving evidence of your existence?

She had more luck in what looked like a combination office and den. Personal photographs were displayed everywhere. An impressive soapstone sculpture of a polar bear in mid-growl, was flanked by framed photos of the whale upstairs posing with other important-looking men. The men in the photos were much like the whale, white and fat and comfortable and certain of their place in the world.

A desk of rich dark wood gleamed in the light streaming through the windows. She opened the top drawer. A pile of letters and bills were addressed to Jason Tremblay. Shanifa couldn't be certain, but she imagined Jason Tremblay was somebody important. An unimportant man would not live in such a big house or have his picture taken with important men.

Or be able to afford young women like herself.

In the bottom drawer, she found a handgun and beneath it a zippered carrying bag. She took the bag out, noting how heavy it was as she placed it on the desktop beside the gun and unzipped it. The bag was stuffed with hundred-dollar bills.

She sat down, staring at the gun and the money. There must be thousands, she thought, suddenly, unreasonably, exhilarated. If she was apprehensive about her future after being in a big house with a rich dead whale in a magical place called Rosedale, well, here was her future. The gun. And the money. The two necessities for survival. The necessities, along with just about everything else, lacking in her young lifetime.

Until now.

Sitting at the desk, not quite believing her good fortune—providing she could keep her head and not do anything stupid that would allow good fortune to slip through her eager fingers—she did not initially hear the sound at the front door.

At first, she thought she was hearing things. But she wasn't. She picked up the gun as she heard the door opening and footsteps coming along the hallway. She shoved the carry case back into the bottom drawer.

A female voice called out, "Jason? I'm here. Where are you?"

Silence for a time. The footsteps resumed, closer. The female voice again, filling with concern this time. "Jason? You did say noon, didn't—"

And a woman was in the doorway, tall with shoulder-length blond hair, wearing a short, flowered summer dress, well-preserved in her late thirties or early forties, Shanifa thought. She pointed the gun in the woman's direction.

The blond woman spoke in a calm, modulated voice: "Where's Jason?"

"Upstairs," Shanifa said.

"Is he all right?"

"He is dead."

The blond woman did not seem perturbed by the news. "Did you kill him?"

Shanifa shook her head.

"That's a Beretta pistol you're holding," the blond woman said. "It belongs to Jason. He keeps it loaded in the bottom drawer of that desk."

Shanifa didn't respond.

"You say Jason's upstairs?"

Shanifa nodded.

"I'd like to see him."

Shanifa rose and came around the desk, keeping the gun leveled at the blond woman.

The blond woman said, "Look, I know what the deal is, okay? I knew he was bringing someone else around today—to share the two of us. I suppose that's you, right?"

Shanifa didn't say anything.

"Today isn't the first time he's done this," the blond woman continued. "He hires me regularly to do these things with him. He's not a bad guy, really."

She paused to allow Shanifa to say something. Shanifa just stood there with the gun. The blond woman gave a helpless shrug. "You don't need the gun. I'm on your side."

Still Shanifa did not respond. The blond woman shrugged again. "Okay, fine. You're a woman of few words. Let me go upstairs, see what we're up against."

At that Shanifa nodded.

Together, they went into the main hall and then up the staircase to the second floor. Shanifa followed the blond woman into the bedroom but held back to allow her to enter the bathroom.

The blond woman was in there long enough to start Shanifa worrying that she was up to something. When she finally emerged, the blond woman's face had become pale. "He's dead all right. It looks like he's had a heart attack. There's blood all over the place from where he hit his head on the tiles." She looked at Shanifa. "Had you and him—"

Shanifa vigorously shook her head.

"That's good," the blond woman said. "You didn't touch the body?"

Shanifa shook her head again.

"Then there's nothing to link you to this. Not unless someone saw you come in the house. Someone other than me, that is." She held out her hand. "I go by the name Maitland, incidentally."

Shanifa lowered the gun and took the offered hand. "Shanifa. Shanifa Mahaba."

Maitland's eyes lit up. "Aha, she talks. And has a name. Okay, Shanifa Mahaba, I'm going to get out of here. I suggest you do the same. There's nothing either of us can do for him. All we can do at this point is get into a lot of shit that involves cops. And I don't think either one of us wants that."

"No," Shanifa said.

"If you don't mind my asking, who brought you here? Someone you can trust?"

Shanifa shrugged. Could she trust Karl? She wasn't sure what that word meant, but she doubted she could trust anyone in her life, certainly not Karl.

"You're not doing this because you want to, are you?" Maitland asked.

Shanifa didn't respond.

"Look, we should both leave. There's a back way out. It leads down into a ravine. Use that. It's not likely anyone will see you. Are you okay with that?"

Shanifa nodded.

"Good luck," Maitland said.

Maitland flashed a brief smile before she swirled out of the room. Shanifa waited a few more minutes and then went downstairs and into the den. She took a deep breath and opened the bottom drawer and pulled out the carry case. She straightened up, noticing that the polar bear soapstone sculpture was no longer on the shelf behind the desk. She had a moment to wonder what had happened to it before she heard something behind her. She turned in time to glimpse Maitland, the soapstone sculpture raised in her hand.

Maitland swung hard, striking the side of Shanifa's head a glancing blow.

She collapsed to the floor, gasping, everything swirling at a dizzying speed.

Then the lights went out.

10

She could hear a voice calling, "Shanifa. For Christ's sake, Shanifa."

Someone was shaking her. Through the buzzing pain in her head—like electric static, she thought—she became aware that she was lying face down on the floor. Something was uncomfortably lodged against her stomach.

The faraway voice called again, sounding closer: "Shanifa."

More shaking. She forced open her eyes to a view of the hulk-like Karl, his pale face set in a mix of concern and anger.

"What the hell," Karl said. "What's going on? What happened to you?"

When Shanifa didn't immediately answer, he shook her harder, intensifying the pain in her head. Bastard, she thought. German bastard.

She stirred on the floor and that was enough to stop the shaking. Karl straightened, standing over her. "Where's the whale?" he demanded. When she didn't answer immediately, his voice became harsher. "Shanifa, where the hell is this guy? What's happened?"

"Upstairs," Shanifa managed to say as she struggled to her knees, seeing that the object pressing against her stomach was the pistol. A gift from Maitland? Bitch,

Shanifa thought. Now Karl had arrived, throwing into disarray any plans she might have had.

"What's he doing up there?"

"Dead," she said.

Karl's face had gone blank with shock. "Dead?" Not quite believing what he was hearing. "What the hell? Did you kill him?"

Shanifa shook her head, creating a wave of pain, everything blurry and indistinct. She felt nauseous, aware of Karl disappearing into the hall. She heard him go up the stairs. It wasn't long before she heard him exclaim, "Shit."

When he came back into the den, she had managed to regain her feet, leaning against the big desk. He stopped when he saw the Beretta in her hand.

"What the hell is that?" he demanded. As if he didn't know, Shanifa thought.

But she didn't say anything. She just held onto the gun. No matter what, she thought, she wasn't going to let go of that gun. If she did, everything was lost.

He advanced toward her. "Did you shoot him? You stupid cow." He slapped her face hard. "Stupid," he repeated.

Her world exploded into a bright red marked by tears springing down her cheeks, the force of the blow rocking her backwards; a lifetime of similar blows, of powerlessness, the inability to do anything but take it—until now.

The pop of the Beretta going off erased the anger on Karl's face, replaced with confusion. "You did not shoot me," he said in a disbelieving voice.

"I did."

She shot him again. He took a couple of steps back looking down at the two holes in his chest.

"*Verdammt*," he breathed and then collapsed to the floor. She stepped over to where he lay on his side. He wasn't moving. Blood had begun to seep from the holes. She stared down at him, considering whether he was dead, not upset about it, although she had to confess this was the first time she had actually killed anyone.

That is if Karl was dead.

If he was, then that could work to her advantage. But if he wasn't dead, it meant more trouble.

She kneeled to put her ear close to Karl's mouth. No sound of breathing, she decided with relief. Blood soaked the front of his shirt.

Shanifa rose to her feet, trying to think what to do next. She looked at the gun in her hand. She wanted to hang onto it; in her world it was wise, as she had just been reminded, to have a weapon that leveled the playing field. Otherwise, she was no more than a young, scared undocumented immigrant with no protection and no advantage. Still, hanging onto the gun she had just used to kill someone had its downside.

She took the Beretta back upstairs and went into the bathroom off the master bedroom. The man—Jason?—lay where she had left him. That wouldn't look good, she thought. She reached in and turned the taps back on. Sprays of water shot across the shower stall. Shanifa used a towel to wipe the taps of possible fingerprints. Then she cleaned the Beretta using the towel and after thinking about it, placed it on the counter beside the sink.

She dropped the towel to the floor and then went to the medicine cabinet and opened it, seeking something that would help her aching head and body. He had a plastic container labelled hydrocodone. She popped two pills into her mouth, replaced the container in the cabinet and then went back into the bedroom.

By the time she got downstairs again, the pain in her head had begun to subside, replaced by a mellowness she hadn't experienced before, a feeling of wellbeing, as though she could get through anything. The effects of the hydrocodone.

She drifted back to the den taking a last look around, everything under control now; Shanifa strong, resolved, infused by a sudden sense of freedom. Smiling to herself, she stepped into the den.

She stopped when she saw the floor.

Karl should have been lying on that floor.

But he wasn't.

11

I don't want to take a dog up there," Mickey said.
"You don't like dogs?" Jean asked.

"I don't like dogs in my car."

"I'll tell you what," Jean said. "The scuba equipment you need is in the back. You can drive out to this quarry by yourself. Feel free to use the equipment."

Mickey grimaced. "Did anyone ever tell you—"

"Don't even think about going there," she warned.

Otis rode proudly in the back of Mickey's SUV.

Mickey turned off the main road and took a number of switchbacks before reaching a gravel road where he slowed and she could see through the trees the waters of the quarry. She could also see a Ford truck backing a boat on a trailer into the water.

"That's Glen," Mickey said. She shot him a look indicating she was not happy to have to deal with Petrusiak. He shrugged and said, "He has the boat."

Mickey parked on the roadside. Otis bounded out of the back of the SUV and then pranced around the roadway, waiting for a sign from Jean that he could run. Mickey helped carry the equipment through the trees, Otis charging ahead to the shore close to where Petrusiak was in his truck backing the boat trailer down to the water. A youthful, dark-haired women in cut-off jeans and a T-shirt gave a cry of delight at Otis's appearance. He came to a stop in front of her, gratefully accepting her pets. "Hey there, fella," the young woman exclaimed. "Where did you come from?"

Cute and sexy, Jean noted. She also noted Mickey's reaction when he saw her, slowing his step, trying not to look surprised, but looking surprised. What was that about? she wondered.

Petrusiak got out of the truck and waved as they approached. "Just in time," he said. "You can help me get the boat in the water, Mickey."

The young woman looked nervous as she eyed Jean. "Hey, Dara," Mickey said. "I want you to meet my friend, Jean Whitlock. Jean, this is Dara Tate. Dara's a constable with the Halton force."

Friend? Jean thought. Well, what else was she? Was she even that? More an acquaintance at this point in their relationship. Relationship? A word she should avoid using, particularly where Mickey was concerned.

Dara managed a smile and said, "Is that handsome fellow your dog?"

"His name is Otis," Jean said. "It looks like you've got a new friend."

"I love dogs," Dara said. She petted a happy Otis some more.

"How long have you been with Halton?" Jean asked.

"Sixteen months," Dara said.

"Long enough for Glen to somehow convince her to marry him," Mickey said.

"Congratulations," Jean said, wondering how Petrusiak had managed to land a hottie like Dara Tate at the same time noting Dara's nervousness and her somewhat peculiar reaction to Mickey busy setting the scuba equipment on the grass.

Glen came over and put his arm around Dara, as if to confirm that he was in fact going to marry her. "Jean doesn't like me," Glen announced.

"That's not true," Jean said, not sounding very convincing.

"For the record, I think this is a crazy idea that's going to get us all in the shitter," Glen said.

"Then why are you doing it, Glen?" Jean asked.

"Because I made him do it," Dara chimed in.

Everyone looked uneasy.

"Well, let's get this done," Jean said.

She went over and inspected her gear that Mickey had unloaded from the SUV: high pressure air tank, regulator, and even a full-face mask that allowed the diver to breathe through the nose. All good, she surmised, and began stripping down to the one-piece bathing suit she wore under her shorts and blouse.

Mickey and Glen got the boat into the water. Dara came over, shy and hesitant. "It's great that you're doing this," she said to Jean. "I just want to say how much I admire you. I mean I've read everything about you, in Maclean's and then your interview on the CBC. You stood strong against those bastards."

"Thanks," Jean said. "But I'm not sure how strong I was."

"Well, you inspired me, you really did. In fact, I joined Halton Police because of you."

"No fair blaming me," Jean said, smiling.

"Seriously, I love it. But I don't think I would have considered police work otherwise."

"Is that where you met Glen?"

"I broke the first rule of police work," Dara said.

"What's that?"

"Never date a cop."

"Yeah, I broke that rule a couple of times myself," Jean said, thinking of Mickey.

"Didn't work out?"

"What can I tell you?"

They traded knowing grins.

Mickey came over, glanced quickly at the two women and then said to Jean, "All set?"

"Just about," Jean said.

She went to work, strapping on her air tank along with the buoyancy control device she had rented. The BCD, as divers called it, allowed her to maintain a constant depth, thus saving energy. She connected the BCD to her tank and then opened the cylinder to make sure air wasn't escaping. Lastly, she attached a weight belt around her waist.

When she had completed her preparations, Mickey held the boat while Jean clambered in. Dara said she would wait on shore, grabbing Petrusiak's arm before he got into the boat and kissing him on the mouth.

"Be back soon, baby," Petrusiak said, pulling away from her.

He got behind the wheel and started up the Mercury outboard engine.

It took only a couple of minutes to reach the middle of the quarry. Petrusiak cut the engine and said, "How's this?"

Jean looked at Mickey. "Any idea what I'm looking for?"

"Something that shouldn't be down there," Mickey said.

Jean positioned herself on the transom strapping her wrist computer into place and then slipped on the fins. "You going to be all right?" Mickey, attempting to reassure himself as much as Jean, actually sounded concerned.

"Heck of a time to ask that question," Jean said. Then seeing his look of consternation, added, "It's like riding a bike—I think."

"Well, be careful."

"Aha, you do care."

"I'm in deep shit if anything happens to you." Mickey grinned.

"We both are," Petrusiak added grimly.

"Then I will do my best to keep you two out of trouble."

"We appreciate that," Mickey said.

She inserted her mouthpiece, made sure that it was working properly, and braced herself, experiencing the wave of fear she always encountered the moment before throwing herself backwards into unknown waters.

The shock hitting surprisingly cold water, almost immediately followed by enveloping warmth as she sank into the murky depths of the quarry. She adjusted the BCD, so that she could control her descent.

When her wrist computer showed a depth of twenty feet, she paused to take in her surroundings. Not that there was much to take in.

At a depth of thirty feet, she could make out the jagged outlines of rocks lining the bottom. At forty-five feet she adjusted her BCD so that she hovered comfortably above rock clusters marking the bottom, skimming along looking for—what, exactly? It remained very much a needle-in-a-haystack situation down here with extremely limited visibility.

After thirty minutes of trailing along the bottom and seeing nothing except her hand in front of her, kicking herself for not insisting on a diving flashlight, she spotted something ahead in the brown haze.

As she drew closer, the outlines of a red Toyota minivan tilted at an angle on the rocks came into view. She reached the side of the van, placed her hand against the cold metal surface. With her free hand she gripped the door handle to steady herself. The driver's-side window was down but there was no one visible inside.

She moved along to the rear, clinging to the fender while she fumbled for the rear door release. The door sprang open in a rush of air and bubbles.

A body floated out, a young woman, her small, pale body suspended in shades of brown and gray. A silver earring trailing a glittering silver fringe dangled from her right ear.

12

Shanifa had only a moment to digest the fact that Karl was not where she left him before Karl reappeared, lunging into view through a second doorway, shirtfront drenched in blood, face twisted in fury, crying out as he threw himself at her.

Shanifa ducked away just in time so that he brushed past her, narrowly missing her, flailing at the air, Shanifa falling against a wall.

Karl came for her again, a raging bull on the attack. Then, as if frozen by some unseen force, Karl suddenly stopped, inches from her. The rage was replaced by confusion as though he heard something far away, God maybe, Shanifa thought, or maybe the devil calling him home.

Karl dropped to the floor, where, as far as Shanifa was concerned, he never should have wasted time leaving in the first place. After all, one way or the other he was bound to die; the best he could have hoped for, she surmised, studying him to make sure he really was dead this time, was to take her with him when he left for whatever his next destination might be.

Except she wasn't going anywhere with Karl.

Finally satisfied that he truly had departed the world, Shanifa allowed herself to breathe again, taking a moment to calm her nerves before she moved over to where Karl lay, knelt down and began to go through his pockets. She found his billfold which contained two hundred dollars in cash—useful—and then his vehicle keys, even more useful.

She stuffed the money in her shoulder bag before taking a last look around. There was no sign of the money she had found in Jason Tremblay's desk. Maitland had taken that after clunking her over the head with the soap sculpture.

An unfortunate mistake on her part, trusting someone she should never have trusted. Breaking her first rule of survival: trust no one.

She made a decision about the Beretta, decided that whatever its drawback, she needed it. She hurried upstairs and retrieved it from the bedroom. Good. She had a gun, some money, and transportation out. Not a bad start, she decided. She was about to leave when she had another thought. Returning to the desk, she went through all the drawers, guessing that if one drawer contained money, maybe another one did too.

No more money but something else. Beneath the bills and receipts, a little black address book that Shanifa promptly dropped into her handbag.

At the front door, she took a moment to calm herself before opening it and exiting into the warmth of the late afternoon. Karl, like a fool, had parked the Dodge van in the drive. Not very discreet. She could run things much better than the idiots who were in charge, the men who had made her life so dreadful. That was fine, she thought, as she got behind the wheel and started the engine. This afternoon she had achieved one of the two things she desired most in this new world in which she found herself: freedom.

She had got off to a fine start achieving her second ambition: revenge.

13

By the time the Ontario Provincial Police divers finished retrieving the body from the waters of the Hidden Quarry, and a crane had been arranged for the following day so the van could be raised, it was growing dark.

Jean, having dressed and stored her scuba gear away in Mickey's SUV, sat with Otis on the rocks above the water, watching as the various police and forensics people who had materialized an hour after Jean discovered the body began slipping away. Everyone came to the homicide party too late, Jean had long since concluded, wanting to be part of the muted excitement of the murder scene but not contributing much other than a presence that signified this was major crime, deserving of attendance.

Below on the narrow shore, officers finished placing the corpse of the young woman into a body bag, Doc Prescott waving his arms, providing direction.

Mickey appeared, causing Otis's head to jerk up, his eyes blazing with suspicion. "There you are," he said. "I wondered where you had gotten to."

"I wasn't being much use down there," Jean said.

"Mind if I join you?"

"Be my guest," she said.

"How does Otis feel about that?"

Otis didn't look happy. Jean ruffled his fur and he relaxed. "He's fine," she said.

Mickey, looking tired, slumped beside her, away from Otis. "How's it going?" she asked.

"They're just packing up," he said.

"Are you okay?"

"I'm in the shitter, of course."

"But you knew that would happen."

"I keep telling myself I don't care. It's results that count. But then I start to care."

"Hey, if you hadn't acted, the other body and the van might never have been discovered."

"Not sure if that's going to make any difference, but we'll see." He gave her a sidelong glance. "Thanks for doing this."

"Three dead women in an abandoned quarry," Jean said.

"What do you think?" asked Mickey.

"Probably the same as you. It's no accident."

"Then who would do something like this?"

"What about the two women you originally found?"

"Young. Asian. Like the woman you found."

"Sex traffickers?"

"You could reach that conclusion," Mickey agreed.

"And have you?"

"I'm not even sure I'm going to be on the case after this afternoon," Mickey said, standing.

She looked up at him. "That's not much of an answer."

"Let's get out of here," he said. "I'll drive you home."

Jean stood to face him. Otis was up and anxious to move on. "There's something I need from you."

"Uh oh. Am I going to have to pay for this afternoon?"

"Information, that's all."

"What kind of information?"

"What you have on a guy named Doyle Parker."

"The name doesn't ring a bell. What has he done?"

"Maybe nothing, but I'd like to know if he's got a record."

"Let me see what I can do."

"One more thing," Jean said.

"Is 'one more thing' going to get me into even bigger trouble?"

"It could. What's with you and Dara?"

Mickey's eyes narrowed. "What?"

"You and Dara."

"She's Glen's fiancée."

"You're very good at not answering questions," Jean said.

"I don't know what you're talking about," he said. "What would make you think there's anything between me and Dara?"

"The looks she kept giving you."

"She wasn't giving me any looks."

"Yes, she was."

"Come on," he said, turning away from her. "I've got to get back to headquarters."

"There's something going on," she called after him as he walked away down the slope. "What is it?"

"You're crazy," Mickey called back.
And kept walking.

14

By seven o'clock that night, Karl still had not returned.

A couple of whales had texted complaining that their young friends were still with them and this was becoming embarrassing. Why hadn't anyone picked them up?

Gail Shirley had been trying to raise the alarm for the past hour, until finally even Dad, who disliked having to confront any sort of reality, acknowledged that something wasn't right. He summoned Doyle Parker to the trailer.

"You haven't heard from Karl by any chance?" Dad inquired.

"Why would I hear from Karl?" Doyle asked.

"Just answer the goddamn question," Gail snapped.

"No ma'am, haven't heard from Karl," Doyle answered in the subdued voice he used when dealing with the Shirleys, the voice that masked the red-hot rage bubbling not far below the surface of his calm.

"You and Karl made the deliveries this afternoon, correct?"

"That's right," Doyle said.

"No problems?"

"Nope. We dropped off the product, then Karl drove me back here. I had some shit to do, so he said he would make the pickups."

"And you saw him drive off?"

"I didn't actually see him, no."

"So you have no idea when he might have left?"

"I was at the compound about four. The van was gone by then."

Gail thought about this before she said, "The whales are calling, complaining that we haven't picked up the product. Everyone except our Rosedale whale."

"Shanifa," Doyle said.

"Karl was supposed to be back an hour ago, but he hasn't shown," Gail said. "We got stranded product. I want you to get into town, fast as you can, stop at Rosedale, make sure everything's all right and then pick up the rest of the product."

Doyle groaned inwardly. The last thing he wanted to do was drive into the city at this time of night to clean up Karl's mess. He gritted his teeth and said, "Sure thing," wondering what the hell had happened.

"I'm going to kill that bastard," Dad Shirley announced to no one in particular.

Gail rolled her eyes. "Let's just get the product and worry about Karl later."

"Maybe something's happened that got things screwed up," Doyle offered. "Could be he's on his way back now."

'If he is, he's not answering his cell," Gail said. She glared at Doyle. "Don't stand there. Get your ass in gear and get moving."

"Yes, ma'am," Doyle said, teeth clenched.

There was something about Shanifa, Doyle thought, the way she looked at you, something that said she knew a whole lot more than she was letting on, that given half a chance she could be a lot of unexpected things, some of them interesting, a lot of them trouble.

Maybe this was the trouble Shanifa had only hinted at before now.

Doyle was thinking about this when he got to Rosedale and started the turn onto the street where they had delivered Shanifa to the whale. Except he couldn't make the turn. Two police cruisers blocked the intersection. Beyond the cruisers, the flashing lights of emergency vehicles brightened the night and cast houses on either side of the street in colors of crimson and yellow.

Not quite believing what he was seeing, holding out faint hope that this wasn't what it looked like, he parked and then hurried back to where a crowd had gathered by the cruisers, prosperous white people not used to police cars flooding their neighborhood.

"Any idea what happened?" Doyle asked of no one in particular.

A sleek, middle-aged woman in jogging shorts said, "Whatever it is, it's going on inside Jason Tremblay's house." As though Doyle should know Jason Tremblay. If the name of the owner didn't mean anything to him, Doyle certainly knew the house, midway along the block, barely visible what with the ambulance and fire truck blocking the view.

"I heard someone broke in," added a teenage girl with silky, waist-length hair that immediately drew

Doyle's attention. He refocused and asked, "Everyone all right?"

"I don't think so," the middle-age woman said. "They brought out a body a few minutes ago."

"They brought out two," someone added.

"This city is falling apart," said a man with a carefully trimmed white mustache and goatee—exactly the sort of jerk that would live in a neighborhood like this, Doyle decided. "Too many guns, that's the problem."

"That's gangbangers," someone else opined. "This is no gangbang, this is Jason for Christ's sake."

What was the big deal about this guy? Doyle wondered irritably. Okay, Jason was one of the bodies. If there were two, who was the other one? Shanifa? Karl?

Who cared about Karl but if it was Shanifa, not only would that mean the end of someone he had the hots for, more seriously it could be the start of a shitstorm that swept him up and dumped him back into prison, a place where he most definitely did not want to end up.

He walked a safe distance away from the onlookers before making the call he dreaded. "We got a problem," Doyle said when Dad Shirley came on the line.

"What kind of problem?" demanded Dad.

"I'm at the Rosedale house where Karl and I dropped Shanifa," Doyle said. "There's no sign of either one of them and the street's full of cops."

"Cops?" Dad said it as though he had never heard the word before.

"The neighbors saw two bodies being carried out of the house."

That drew silence on the other end of the line. "Dad?"

"Yeah, I'm here. What about the other girls?"

"This is my first stop. Like I was told."

"Is Karl's vehicle there?"

"No idea," Doyle replied. "The cops have the street blocked off so I can't see much."

More silence and then: "All right, get out of there, pick up the others and then get your ass back here."

"Roger that," Doyle said.

15

"Let's not frigging panic," Gail Shirley said after her husband got off the phone and began cursing loudly.

"I'm not goddamn panicking." Dad Shirley, sounding like he was panicking. "But this sure as hell doesn't look good, and, if it's as bad as I think it is, then what?"

"First of all, let's get the facts," Gail said quietly. She was at her laptop, working at the keyboard. "Let's find out what happened."

"Two dead bodies. Jesus Christ," Dad said. "That's Jason Tremblay, right?"

"We thought he'd like Shanifa." Gail peered at the computer screen.

"*We* thought? I had nothing to do with this. That goddamn kid who never said anything. I caught her a couple of times giving me the stink eye. If something's happened, she's involved, I'll bet."

"Maybe she gave you the stink eye because you wouldn't keep your hands off her," Gail offered, working the keyboard of her laptop.

"I never touched that goddamn woman," Dad protested.

"Yeah sure," Gail said. "So far there's nothing online."

"Doesn't mean shit," Dad said. "It's early, that's all." He shook his head and then hobbled across the room to his recliner. "If something's happened to Tremblay, Christ, that's gonna be big news."

Gail hit some more keys and then stiffened. "Okay, here's something. Canadian Press is reporting that police have removed two bodies from the home of former Minister of Defense Jason Tremblay. So far, they're not identifying the bodies, but neighbors believe one of the dead is Tremblay."

"Shit," Dad said, slumping into the recliner.

Gail noted his heavy breathing and thought again that he wasn't going to be much help when it came to dealing with a crisis. Useless, when it came down to it.

By the time Doyle picked up the stranded product and arrived back at the quarry, it was late and Dad was sound asleep in his chair; the old man snoring, Gail thought disdainfully.

She had waited by the phone hoping against hope that Karl would call. But there was no call.

The product, meanwhile, looked tired and frightened.

Gail sat the five down and got them water. Doyle, arms folded, leaned against the trailer wall watching intently. "Did Shanifa say anything to any of you?" Gail asked.

The women traded worried, helpless glances.

"Anything about what she might do when she got to Toronto?"

"Do?" Kiva looked more confused. "What she *do*?"

"They told me on the way out here that Shanifa didn't talk to them," Doyle interjected. "Shanifa never says shit to anybody. Pretty much keeps to herself."

Gail kept her eyes on the women. "I'm not asking you, Doyle. I'm asking them."

To Doyle, the women resembled deer caught in headlights or, more accurately, in the glare of Gail's laser focus, a glare that unsettled him when he was on the receiving end of it, let alone what it would do to these kids.

"Shanifa didn't like it here," Amber managed to say.

"As opposed to the rest of you," Gail said with a shrug.

The women looked at her blankly.

Gail shifted her gaze to Doyle. "What about Karl?"

"What about him?"

"Any sense that he might do something really stupid with one of our whales?"

Doyle shrugged. "I dunno. Karl is a mean son of a bitch, but I don't know that he's into killing rich guys in Toronto."

Gail rose and went over to where Dad was snoring softly and gave him a poke. The old man came awake with a loud grunt. "What the hell?" he exclaimed. When he saw Gail looming over him, his face darkened. "I thought I told you not to do that," he growled.

"I need you to stay awake, you old bastard."

Dad gave a hot-eyed glare aimed at the others in the room. Dad made Doyle just about as nervous as Gail did. A couple of poisonous snakes these two. Dangerous at any time; particularly dangerous when cornered.

And right now, they appeared to be cornered.

"Yeah, I'm awake, woman," Dad said, "but it don't change the fact there's not much we can do except get these gals back to where they belong, with our friend Cai, and then lay low until we see how this plays out."

"Cai Mak is not going to like that one bit," Gail countered. "He's gonna say what's obvious: the whales call. No way is he gonna let us shut down."

Dad struggled to his feet, leaning hard on his cane. Doyle moved to help him. Dad angrily waved him away. "Stay back! I don't need no one's help." He hobbled over to face Gail, his eyes small black pools of anger.

"To hell with him. What does he know? You do as I say. We stand down."

"And I say we can't do that," Gail replied.

With his free hand, the one that wasn't grasping his cane, Dad slapped Gail across the face, a resounding whack that echoed through the room. One of the women, Doyle didn't see who, let out an involuntarily yelp, as though she was the one who had been hit.

Gail's head was snapped to one side by the force of the blow. She rocked back, holding her hand to her face. The two glowered at each other, full of mutual hate, Doyle thought, two people hating each other's guts, yet locked together for survival.

As though Dad could tell what he was thinking, he swung around to Doyle and snapped out an order, "Get these gals the hell out of here."

16

If she had a nice place to live, a safe house where she could escape from everything, Shanifa would never give out that address to a whale, certainly not a whale who would then write it down in a little book for anyone with any brains to find.

But Maitland was stupid or at least not smart enough, Shanifa concluded. That was fine. The carelessness of others only worked to her advantage. Therefore, finding where Maitland lived was no more difficult than consulting Jason Tremblay's black address book and then plugging the house number into the GPS built into Karl's Dodge.

A house on Acacia Road, a pleasant northern section of the city. It was not what she expected: two stories, a brick façade, a swatch of neatly trimmed lawn surrounded by hedges. A stoop with an iron railing led to an entrance door, tiny windows surrounding a brass knocker.

You could mount those steps and use the knocker to announce your presence, as simple as that. Everything in this country was so simple. People were trusting fools who carelessly left their things around, money and guns—and addresses. Life was hard here for someone like her, no question. But paradoxically it was also easy once you decided to take action. There were many ways of escape.

And lots of ways into the places you wished to access—like taking the broken and cracked concrete walkway at the side of Maitland's house and following it around to the back where peeling steps led to a rotting deck and sliding glass door conveniently left open. Beyond the door was a kitchen where the blond woman who called herself Maitland, in sweats and without makeup, leaned forward to insert a spoonful of something into the mouth of an elderly woman with a shock of white hair slumped in a wheelchair.

Maitland started as Shanifa came in from the stoop with the Beretta. Then, with seeming calm, Maitland gently wiped the old woman's chin using the napkin she held. The old woman smiled appreciatively and then gazed at Shanifa with milky, uninterested eyes.

"This is my mother, Hafsa," Maitland said. "She's visiting this afternoon from the senior residence where she lives." She fed her mother another spoonful of what looked like soup. "Mom, this is a friend of mine from work."

Hafsa appeared not to hear her daughter. Maitland said, "Mom's had some health issues lately, but she's doing really good. Aren't you, Mom?"

Hafsa sat, head down a bit, staring into some faraway space that Shanifa suspected only Hafsa could reach.

"I want my money," Shanifa said. She moved further into the kitchen, not taking any chances, staying alert to any possibility, careful not to be distracted a second time by Maitland's apparent calmness.

"How did you know where to find me?" Maitland put the spoon down on the table.

"My money," Shanifa repeated.

"That bastard Jason," Maitland said. "I suppose he wrote down my address in his book. I told him not to do that, but I guess he didn't listen, and you, it turns out, are a lot smarter than I gave you credit for."

Shanifa didn't respond, keeping her gaze on Maitland.

"Look, the money's upstairs, okay? I'll get it for you, no problem. I shouldn't have whacked you over the head, I'm sorry about that."

Maitland paused to see if Shanifa would respond and when she didn't, she continued. "You want to know what I think? I don't think you're going to shoot me and my mother. It's not worth it. I suspect you're hooked up to one of the services Jason used occasionally. You work for Cai Mak's people, right? I know Cai. He got me started in the business. Jason probably wanted to do us together." She smiled. "The thought of the two of us was too much for him. That probably killed him."

"Give me my money," Shanifa said.

Maitland grimaced impatiently "Look, I'm going to give you the money, no worries. But I want to suggest something to you. Okay?"

Shanifa remained unresponsive.

"Unless I miss my guess, Cai's people have their claws into you. That money in Jason's house could be the way out for you. I understand, and I'll give it to you. But you need help. Am I right about that?"

Shanifa failed to hide the look that told Maitland she was right.

"I can provide the help you need," Maitland went on. "I'm a freelancer. I work for myself. That means I don't have people keeping me prisoner, taking my money. No asshole men to deal with, except of course"—another smile—"the whales. And some of them aren't so bad."

Shanifa thought about what this woman was saying. Not that Shanifa felt that this Maitland could be trusted, even as she sat feeding her sick mother, but right now there weren't a lot of alternatives.

"You should know something," Maitland said.

Shanifa cocked her head.

"You're beautiful," Maitland went on. "You can do a whole lot better than what they've probably made you do, Shanifa Mahaba. Where do you come from?"

Shanifa hesitated before she said, "Kenya."

"You're a long way from home."

Shanifa nodded. "I was taken in the town where I grew up. They told me I would marry a rich man. Then they moved me to Dubai. They told me I would marry a rich man. And then here. Canada."

Maitland couldn't help but smile. "Did they say you would marry a rich man?"

"Not in Canada. No. By the time I came here I knew better than to believe anything."

Shanifa wasn't smiling.

"Well, believe this," Maitland said. "You're safe here."

"I am safe nowhere," Shanifa asserted. "That is why I am still alive."

"I can tell you this," Maitland said. "You may not marry a rich man but with me you will be able to screw them and in return they will pay you a lot of money. How does that sound?"

Shanifa thought about this and then lowered the gun. "You have the money?"

Maitland said, "It's upstairs."

"Get it."

"You still don't trust me."

Shanifa just looked at her.

"All right. All right. Wait here."

She went out of the kitchen. Shanifa didn't move. She stared at Maitland's mother. Maitland's mother stared back at her.

Maitland returned with the carry bag and placed it on the counter beside Shanifa.

"Now will you put the gun away?"

17

A pale face floated through the gloom, a haunted face, eyes wide with fear, a look of pure terror the moment before death, knowing for certain it's coming and cannot be stopped.

The image that sat just behind Jean's eyes; the image she could not shake, demanding recognition.

She telephoned Doc Prescott. He should have told her to get lost, that she was no longer in an official capacity that would allow her to ask any questions, but they had known each other too long for that. She came from a family of undertakers. Her father had owned one of the town's two funeral homes. She had been groomed for the business, had grown up with death and Doc Prescott sharing a rye and ginger ale after work with her father.

So Doc didn't tell her to get lost. Instead, he told her to come around. He had just finished the autopsy on the young woman.

"Female, obviously, Asian, also obviously. Five feet two inches tall, ninety-five pounds. Black hair. Brown eyes. All the things easily ascertained."

Doc Prescott still in his protective scrub suit stood beside the metal table on which the body of the young woman was laid out, wrapped in a plastic shroud, an ethereal presence now, like something drawn from a tomb in a bad adventure movie.

"Did they find any identification?" Jean asked.

"The police didn't find anything in the van, and, of course, there was nothing on the women."

"Except a silver earring," Jean amended.

"Not very helpful," Doc said with a shrug.

"Unless you can find the other earring."

"Well, they didn't find it in the van," Doc said. "Probably at the bottom of that quarry."

"What about cause of death? Have you reached any conclusions?"

"Ascertaining whether a victim has drowned, as you probably know, is a process of elimination," Doc explained. "You rule out other possible causes of death, which is why we do an autopsy."

"And so?"

"I've ruled out anything else that might have killed our three victims. They were trapped in a car under-water. Inhaled water entered the alveolar spaces of the lungs, making it difficult as the victim struggles for oxygen to enter the bloodstream. As the oxygen is deplet-ed from the bloodstream, the victim loses conscious-ness in as little as three minutes, and that is that.

"The problem," Doc continued, "is ascertaining what caused the drowning. Was it accidental or was foul play involved? That's where the other causes of death come into play and thus far, I haven't been able to find anything."

"Except I found this person jammed into the back of a van at the bottom of a quarry," Jean said, nodding at the body on the table.

He made a gesture with his hands. "You never know. Your victim has contusions on her body, but they could have been caused by her attempts to escape when the van went into the water. The other two women could have been transporting the woman in the back, made a wrong turn and the three ended up in the quarry, unable to escape."

"Seems highly unlikely," Jean said.

"Highly unlikely is the name of the game I constantly play," Doc Prescott said.

"About as unlikely as finding you here," a voice behind Jean said.

She turned to see Mickey Dann entering the autopsy room, not looking happy. Doc Prescott made a face. "Jean's an old friend. She dropped around to say hello."

"Yeah, I'm sure," Mickey said.

"I was just on my way out," Jean said. She gave Doc a hug. "Good to see you, Doc. Say hi to Sarah for me."

"She wants to have you over for dinner soon," Doc said.

"That would be great. Give me a call."

Jean went out into the parking lot, Mickey following. "You're not stalking me, are you?" she asked.

"Hardly."

"Then what are you doing?"

"Trying to keep you out of trouble—as usual."

"I found that woman in there," Jean said. "Obviously, I have an interest in what happened to her."

"You need a hobby," he said.

"I'm raising a dog," Jean said as she reached her vehicle.

"And sticking your nose in where it doesn't belong," Mickey said. "In case you've forgotten, you're no longer a police officer."

"I was thinking the same thing when I was forty feet down in that quarry with a dead body floating past me."

"Okay, I appreciate what you did, you know that," Mickey said.

"Do I? You've got a funny way of showing your appreciation."

"Look, I asked you for a favor and you were great, and like I say, I appreciate it, but that's as far as it can go. Otherwise, you're going to get us both into trouble. And more trouble is what I don't need right now."

"What about Doyle Parker?" she asked.

That caused him to pause and take a breath. "That's the other thing. Why are you so interested in him?"

"Then you looked him up," Jean said.

"A low-level dipshit as far as I can see, a couple of break-and-enter charges when he was a kid. He pleaded guilty to one. The other was dropped. He was also arrested a couple of years ago for assaulting someone in a bar, but those charges were eventually dismissed. The Mounties charged him in with trafficking in persons and living off the avails of prostitution, but those charges were also dropped and that brings me to the reason for this visit."

"Aha. There is a reason."

"Something I'd like you to do for me."

"Should I get my scuba gear out again?"

"I'd like you to stay away from Doyle."

"Why would you like me to do that?"

"This doesn't come from me. It comes from your old friends at the RCMP."

"You're kidding."

"No sooner did I start to ask around about him then I get a call saying lay off."

"Why?"

"Your guess is as good as mine," Mickey said. "But this comes from the top, and I'm already in trouble with the top so I'd like you to help me out here. Spend more time with your dog, and a lot less time getting tangled up in police activities."

"Thanks for the advice," she said.

"You know I like you," he said.

His words came abruptly, catching her off guard.

"I don't know anything of the sort," she said.

"You make it hard," he said.

"Do I?"

"Yeah, you do."

Jean opened the driver's-side door and got in. As she drove out, she glanced in the rearview mirror. She could see Mickey in the parking lot.

Not moving.

18

By the time she reached the Hidden Quarry the following afternoon, Jean had convinced herself that Mickey was only doing his job and that he was right about already being in enough trouble without her nosing around. But then he was the one who had talked her into the dive in the first place; rekindled instincts she would just as soon have left dormant. Now those instincts had drawn her back to stand above the water-filled pit beneath a threatening afternoon sky.

It's your fault, Mickey, she told herself. Your fault that I can't resist one more look around the quarry, if nothing else to allay her suspicion that not enough was being done by these male cops to get to the bottom of what had happened to three anonymous women.

She made her way through the field above the quarry, taking note of the adjacent roadway, the distant woods. The van could have come along here at night, the driver misjudging the cliff edge, plunging over into the water. But then how was it the two women were nude? And how did that explain the body in the back?

"Everything all right?"

Jean swung around to find a man emerging from the trees, walking toward her. A baseball cap shaded a narrow, fortyish face and a sparse beard. A checked red shirt was tucked into baggy jeans.

"Just admiring the view," Jean said.

"Sorry to bother you," the man said. "You looked a little lost. It happens around here. People don't expect to encounter this—" His sweeping hand took in the expanse of the quarry. "It tends to throw folks."

"No, I'm okay."

"Glad to hear it." He leaned forward, offering his hand. "Jim Callahan."

"Jean," Jean said, taking his offered hand.

"I'm around this area quite a bit. Breaking trails for my hiking group."

"Breaking trails?"

"Working out hiking routes, making sure nothing's too challenging for those of us of a certain age."

"It's a spectacular landscape," Jean said.

"They closed this quarry about ten years ago," Jim Callahan said. "Finally ran the Shirleys out of here, thank God."

"The Shirleys?"

"They owned this quarry and another smaller one down the road. They were digging way beyond the allowed depth, endangering the town's water supply before the province finally put a stop to it. However, they still work a second pit, and who knows what they're up to there."

"So they aren't far from here," Jean said, turning to peer back at the roadway.

"Couple of miles, if that," Jim said. "Not much of an operation anymore. These days, the big corporate guys run most of the quarries, but the Shirleys for whatever reason hang in there."

"You don't like them?"

Jim Callahan shrugged. "Gail and her husband, Dad. Real characters. Most of the pits around here, they give us access so we can hike across their properties. Not the Shirleys. They keep us out. They've even got security over there making sure we stay away."

"Did you know they found three bodies here in the quarry?"

He looked surprised and then shook his head. "I've been canoeing in Algonquin Park for the past two weeks. Just got back. I came out here today to plan our weekly hike. Any idea what happened?"

"Three young women. Their van was found at the bottom of the quarry," Jean said. "Police aren't sure if it was an accident."

"That's terrible," Jim Callahan said, sounding shocked. "Really weird."

"Why weird?" Jean asked.

"Well, why would they drive a van along the road? Where would they be going?"

"Maybe, like me, they heard about this place and came out to have a look."

Jim Callahan eyes narrowed. "You're not from the police by any chance?"

"Just an interested onlooker," Jean said. "Why? Are you on the run from the law?"

Jim laughed. "Yeah, I'm hiding out. Please don't tell anyone you found me."

"Your secret is safe," Jean said.

"Seriously," Jim went on, "the big quarries sometimes hire off-duty cops as security to keep people away, particularly the people who don't like the idea of more quarries."

"Are you one of those people?"

Jim nodded. "There's an application before the municipality to reopen what they call an 'aggregate extraction operation,' in other words another quarry about five miles away. I'm on a committee fighting that application."

"Are there a lot of quarries in this area?"

"Too many as far as I'm concerned. This proposed quarry, for example. They love the limestone they can take out, but it screws up the environment, adds to an overburdened traffic flow, and generally makes life miserable for local residents, not to mention the potential damage to the water table—the water we all drink."

"A worthy cause, obviously," Jean said.

"Listen, all my blathering about quarries aside, I'm actually a fairly entertaining guy."

"Glad to hear it."

"After one of these trail breaks, as I call them, I usually go to this little place called the Union Market Square in Arkell. Just a roadside place, but they serve great coffee and the desserts are fantastic. I wonder, you know, two lost souls out here at the Hidden Quarry, would you be interested in joining me?"

"Are you a lost soul, Jim?" Jean asked.

"Metaphorically speaking," Callahan said, grinning.

Jean thought about it for a moment and then said, "And you're entertaining?"

"I try my best."

"In that case, sure, metaphorically speaking, why not?"

———————

Jim Callahan was right about the coffee and the delightful little roadside café that was the Union Market Square. And the pecan pie they shared wasn't so bad, either.

"There are some great trails around here if you're ever in the mood," Jim said, once they had succeeded in devouring the pie and now lingered over their coffees.

"Yeah?" Jean said, trying to summon an interest in hiking trails.

"There is the Arkell Springs Trail that runs along the Eramosa River. The Starkey Hill Loop is just east of here."

"You do a lot of that? Hiking—in addition to fighting for a better world?"

"When I'm not fighting for a better world, I've been known to wander along a trail or two in my time," Jim said with a grin. "What about you?"

"I'm afraid I don't fight much for a better world, but I do walk a dog around the Mill Pond in Milton," Jean said.

"Is that what you do for a living? Walk dogs?"

She laughed and said, "Sometimes it feels that way. But no, that's not what I do professionally. What about you?"

"I left the Ministry of Natural Resources and Forestry six months ago."

"What did you do there?"

"I was a geographer and water resources guy," he said.

"Now you're retired?"

"Let's say I'm at a time in my life when I'm looking for something else."

"Have you found it?" Jean asked.

"Found what?"

"The elusive something else. Or does trying to stop quarries from being built do it for you?"

"Not quite, I'm afraid," he said with another grin. "However, I am still looking."

"Along hiking trails."

"Yeah, could be," he said. He took a sip of his coffee. "But you still haven't answered my question."

"What was your question?"

"I believe it was along the lines of what you do for a living."

"Right. *That* question." She paused. "Let's see. Maybe I'm spending my time in search of that elusive something else."

"Two souls, searching," Jim said.

She thought about that and then said, "Yes, maybe you're right."

Finally, the pie was gone and there was no more coffee and they drifted outside and stood by the rattle-trap red pickup truck he had arrived in. Jean couldn't help pondering as they shook hands whether she could date a guy who drove a pickup truck.

"That's some truck you've got there," she said.

"It's a piece of shit," he said. "But it's my piece of shit."

"Aren't you polluting the environment with that thing?"

"I'm afraid you've probably right. You have found my Achilles' heel."

"Aha."

"If you ever decide you want to try something other than the Mill Pond, give me a call." He handed her a white business card. It contained his name, phone number and an address in Georgetown.

She looked at him. "Georgetown?"

"The outskirts," he said. "A crappy truck, a house in Georgetown. Deal breakers?"

"Not necessarily," she said.

"There's hope?"

"There's always hope," Jean said. "Besides, a cousin of mine lives in Georgetown."

"There you go," he said. "I'm not even going to ask her name or his name. I only bought the house six months ago."

"About the time you left the Ministry."

About the time," he said with another one of his grins. She was beginning to like those smiles.

"If I'm up in that area…" she allowed the sentence to trail off, not sure where she might take it.

"There are some great trails around Georgetown, too."

"Good to know."

They stood awkwardly for a minute or two longer. "I'd better get going," he said.

"Me too," she said.

For a crazy moment she had an inclination to kiss him. But then he was behind the wheel of the shitty truck that sounded even worse than it looked as he drove away.

She walked to her vehicle pondering the notion of dating a guy in a pickup truck.

She could do it, she decided. What the hell. He was cute.

Kind of cute.

19

For most of the first night Shanifa kept the gun beside her and hardly slept at all. Toward morning, she finally dropped into a deep sleep. It was like turning off a light switch. One moment she was there, the next she was gone.

She awoke at eight a.m. The gun lay where she had left it. She was still alive. The carry bag was still under the bed where she had placed it.

Since Maitland hadn't killed her in the night or stolen the money when she had the chance, maybe it was going to be all right. Not that she trusted Maitland; she didn't trust anyone. But for now, maybe Maitland was right. If she could not marry a rich man, she would sleep with rich men and make money.

She spent the next half hour counting the cash in the carry bag. There was one hundred and five thousand dollars, mostly one hundred-dollar bills, but also a half dozen five hundred-dollar bills, too.

She was rich, she concluded, stuffing the cash back into the carry bag. Rich, that is, if she could hang onto the money. That was the trick was it not? To somehow keep it from the murderers and the thieves.

Yes, she thought, that would be the trick all right.

———

Maitland's real name, it turned out, was Adara Dunia. "Adara means virgin, if you can believe it," she told Shanifa with a laugh. Her family was from Iraq. Her father had deserted her and her mother and brother when she was only ten. Her brother suspected what she was doing and had disowned her. Her mother, Hafsa, had been diagnosed with early dementia. Maitland was her sole support; she had to keep working in order to pay for the senior residence where Hafsa lived when she was not with her daughter.

Shanifa decided that she liked Maitland, although she didn't like the fact that she smoked. Maitland would slip off to the deck with her pack of Dunhill cigarettes, leaning against the railing, looking out into the neighbors' backyards. She would light one of her cigarettes, inhale deeply, and for a moment at least, appear at peace with herself.

There was one other thing that Shanifa disliked, that made her suspicious of Maitland: her habit of promptly closing her cellphone the moment Shanifa came into view. She said nothing about it, but she took note; Maitland was not entirely what she seemed.

"Jason was remote and sort of quietly kinky, my best client," Maitland explained to Shanifa. "My very best when I think about it. Did I tell you he was a former member of parliament?"

Shanifa shook her head, not sure what that meant.

"Very important guy. A minister of some sort in the Conservative government. Used to be a minister. Since I've known him, he's been retired."

She inhaled deeply on her second Dunhill of the evening. "Listen, he's not the only high-end whale out there. If we do this right, there are lots of similar whales willing to pay big money. We just have to find them. First of all, though, there are problems we need to solve."

"What problems?"

Maitland doused her cigarette and said, "I'm not sure where you got that van of yours but it's probably hot and we should get rid of it. Okay?"

Shanifa's look was uncertain. Giving up that vehicle was tantamount to giving up her gun, maybe worse. The loss of the easy way of escape.

"I've got my car so there is transportation when needed," Maitland hastened to add. "It's a Ford Eco-Sport, no big deal. But it doesn't attract attention, either. Believe me, if this works out, in a few weeks you'll be able to buy just about anything you want."

Shanifa considered this, trying to see the wisdom in it. "For now, I can use your car?"

"Whenever you want," Maitland said.

Shanifa nodded and said, "Okay."

Later that evening, as it was growing dark, Shanifa followed Maitland's red Ford north to Highway 401 and the cutoff for a place called Brampton. Shanifa, despite herself, grew increasingly nervous. If the van was hot, as Maitland said, then here she was totally exposed on a major highway.

But then they were on backroads and Shanifa began to relax as she tracked Maitland's taillights for an hour through farm country until they reached a town called Belfountain.

Up a hill and then down into an overgrown lane. Finally, Maitland pulled over to the side. Shanifa parked behind her, and in the glare of Shanifa's headlights, Maitland got out and came back to the driver's-side window. "Put it in the laneway there," she ordered. "I've got some Mr. Clean and some dust cloths. We'll wipe the car down and leave it here. Is that okay?"

"I have no idea where we are," Shanifa said.

"That's all right," Maitland said. "All you need to know is that it's a long way from any place the cops can associate with us. Here." She pushed a pair of blue rubber kitchen gloves through the open window to Shanifa. "Let's do it."

They turned off the headlights of the two cars and then worked in darkness for the next hour using Mr. Clean Freak—*Deep Cleaning Mist*— going over every inch of the interior. Windex cleaned the windows inside and out.

When they had finished, Maitland locked the vehicle, crossed the laneway and heaved the keys away into the darkness of an adjacent field.

On the way back, Shanifa studied Maitland, alternating light and shadow from oncoming traffic shifting across her intense face. "Why are you doing this?" she asked.

"Doing what?"

"Helping me," Shanifa said.

"Don't people help you?"

"No," came the prompt reply.

Maitland couldn't help but laugh. "Boy, you really are a wounded warrior, aren't you? I guess we both are. I see a lot of you in me—two women who've been dealt a bad hand, but who can work together and help one another."

Shanifa considered this, riding along in the darkness, and then she opened her bag, moved the Beretta to one side and withdrew the address book she had taken from Jason Tremblay's desk. She laid it on the console between them.

Maitland allowed herself a glance at it. "What's that?"

"The men we need. The men who will help us to help each other," Shanifa said.

20

Maitland saw the car parked in front of her house as she turned into the drive.

Two figures came down from the stoop. Maitland grabbed the address book and shoved it under the seat, saying to Shanifa, "Let me handle this."

"Who are they?" Shanifa asked.

"Nobody good," Maitland replied opening the door and getting out.

By the time, Shanifa slid out the passenger side, a man and a woman were confronting Maitland. The woman was fat and blond, Shanifa noted. The man had a hard, lived-in face she didn't like.

The fat woman showed Maitland a badge. Shanifa heard her say, "Maitland, we're from the Toronto Police. I'm Detective Sergeant Dash Jessup. This is my partner, Detective Bing Farley."

"How are you tonight, Maitland?" Bing Farley asked politely.

Maitland made sure not to look nonplussed by the presence of the two detectives. She said, "What can I do for you?"

"Can we talk inside, Maitland?" the detective sergeant named Jessup asked.

Maitland shook her head. "My mother's ill and sound asleep. Let's talk out here."

Dash looked over at Shanifa. "Who's your friend?"

"A friend," Maitland replied curtly. "What do you want?"

"Do you know a man named Jason Tremblay?"

"Should I?"

Dash Jessup made an impatient face. "Come on, Maitland, don't play games. It's late and I want to get home to my children."

"Then go home, Sergeant," she said. "I don't have to answer these questions."

"Tell you what, Maitland." This was Bing Farley interjecting himself. "Why don't we put you in that car over there and take you down to the station? You can call your lawyer from there and then we can have a formal interrogation rather than a friendly conversation."

"Jason Tremblay is a friend," Maitland stated.

"When was the last time you saw him?"

"It's been a while," Maitland said. "Why do you ask?"

"When you say, 'it's been a while?' How long would that be?" Dash asked.

"In fact, I dropped around to his house last week, but either he wasn't home or he wasn't answering his door. Does that count as seeing him?"

Bing Farley had produced a notebook, and was using a pen to scribble in it.

"What day was this last week?" Jessup demanded.

"Wednesday, I think." Maitland paused, as though trying to remember. "Yes, Wednesday. Jason had called to see how I was doing. I was passing by and decided to stop. But like I say, no one answered the door."

"And that was it? You just left?"

"That's right."

"And you didn't see anything suspicious?"

"I'm not sure what you mean by suspicious."

"Suspicious. Out of the ordinary."

"Other than the fact he wasn't answering the door, no. Nothing."

Farley stepped in at that point. "Here's the thing, Maitland. A neighbor says she saw you coming out of Jason Tremblay's house on Wednesday. This is the day his body was found upstairs in his bedroom."

"I have no idea what this person is talking about," Maitland said. "The neighbor may have seen me leaving but I didn't get in the door." She gave the two detectives a mystified look that impressed Shanifa. "What do you mean about Jason's body?"

"Have you been watching the news lately?" Jessup asked.

Maitland shook her head. "I've been busy with my mother. Is Jason dead?"

"His body was found the day the neighbor says you were in his house."

"I told you, I wasn't *in* his house," Maitland said. "I adored Jason. If I was inside and something happened to him, I would have called an ambulance."

"The neighbor heard what sounded like a gunshot. That's when she called police. When officers arrived, they found Jason Tremblay in the shower. Downstairs, they found the body of a second man, dead from gunshot wounds. Do you know anything about that?"

Shanifa wondered if that revelation might cause Maitland to look spontaneously over at her, thus complicating things even more than they were. But to Maitland's credit, she was satisfied to look genuinely shocked while keeping her eyes on the police officers.

"I don't understand," was all she could say. "There was another man in the house with Jason?"

"That's correct," Dash said. "You didn't hear a gunshot?"

"No, of course not. Was Jason shot?"

"It doesn't look like it," Farley said. "But we're looking for more information. That's why we're hoping you can help us."

"I don't know anything more than I've told you," Maitland said. Her voice resonated truthfully, thought Shanifa. Maitland had left before Karl arrived; there was nothing for her to tell but the truth.

Maybe it was Shanifa's intense focus on Maitland, but that was the moment she caught the eye of the detective named Bing Farley. "What about your friend?" he demanded, jerking a thumb in Shanifa's direction.

"She's helping me with my mother," Maitland said dully.

"What's your name?" Bing Farley called to her.

"Her name's Shanifa."

"Are you in the business, too?"

Shanifa looked at him blankly.

"I told you," Maitland snapped. "She's a caregiver, helping me with my mother. None of this involves her."

Dash Jessup gave Shanifa a long look, suspicion mixed with—what? Attraction? Could be, Shanifa thought. The look evaporated as Dash returned to

Maitland, producing a business card. "We're going to let this go for now," she said. "But we may have more questions later. Meanwhile, if you think of anything, Maitland, give me a call at that number. Okay?"

Maitland accepted the card, saying nothing. Only when the detectives start walking away, did she allow herself to glance at Shanifa.

Not a friendly glance, Shanifa thought.

No sooner were they settled inside than Maitland left to tend to her mother at the senior residence. She was gone for over an hour, longer than usual, probably because she didn't want to deal with Shanifa. At least that's what Shanifa surmised sitting quietly in the living room, arms folded, trying not to think of anything, simply enjoying the silence, the sensation, however transitory, of comfort and safety.

Even if Maitland wasn't speaking to her.

She heard the click of Maitland's heels returning through the kitchen, heard her opening and closing the refrigerator, the sound of a tap being turned on in the sink. Finally, Maitland appeared in the living room, holding a glass of white wine. She looked grim as she moved to seat herself on the edge of the sofa facing Shanifa.

"I'm really pissed at you," Maitland said.

Shanifa acknowledged that with a nod of her head.

"I know your whole thing is not to say much," Maitland continued, "but not telling me what went on at Jason's after you left, to stay silent when you knew the cops would be investigating, when it was only a matter of time before they showed up at *my* door, I mean, Jesus Christ, what were you thinking?"

Shanifa was thinking that this woman had knocked her unconscious and left her lying on the floor; that if that hadn't happened, she would have been out of the house long before Karl arrived; that she had little choice but to shoot him. It was a matter of survival. It was always a matter of survival. But someone like Maitland would never understand that so Shanifa was not about to waste her breath.

She was aware that Maitland was still talking and refocused her attention. "At the very least we should get rid of the gun. That's the murder weapon, I assume."

Murder weapon? Shanifa thought. The gun was keeping her alive, the protection she would otherwise not have in this strange North American jungle in which she now found herself.

"I will keep the gun," Shanifa said.

"The police find you with that gun and you go to jail for the rest of your life," Maitland said. "And I won't be far behind you."

Shanifa didn't say anything. She could see that Maitland was working to contain her anger.

"Are you just going to sit there and not speak?" Maitland demanded.

"We will need the gun," Shanifa said.

"Why? Why do we need the gun?"

"For what we are going to do."

"And what is it we're going to do, exactly?"

"We are going to be rich," Shanifa pronounced.

"The gun will not make us rich," Maitland countered.

"The gun will stop the people who would stop us from becoming rich," Shanifa countered.

21

Doyle had sat outside for the past four hours and there had been nothing, except finally as it grew dark, lights flaring inside Daye's Georgetown house.

Correction, Doyle thought, *his* goddamn Georgetown house.

He was ready to give up for the night when the cream-colored BMW sedan came along, slowed and then drove on to the end of the block and pulled over to the curb.

A tall dude in jeans and an open-neck white shirt got out, carrying a bottle of wine. He came along the street, cocky as you please, pausing in front of Daye's house—*his* house for Christ's sake—before climbing the front steps like he goddamned owned the place, which he most certainly did not. That was *his* house. *His goddamn wife.*

The door opened and he caught a glimpse of Daye before she stepped back to allow the dude inside. The door closed and the street resumed its silence. Except inside his truck, Doyle screamed silently, his head exploding with dark images of what was going on inside that house—*his goddamn house*—his wife, kissing that dude, drinking his red wine, taking off her clothes—

His hands gripped the steering wheel, his whole body coiled in fury. The screaming inside his head drowned out what he was thinking. What he didn't want to think. What he couldn't think.

He lurched out of the truck, needing air, taking deep breaths. He marched along the street, cursing to himself, full of black thoughts about what he would do about the dude with the bottle of wine; the dude in the house—*his* house for Christ's sake!—screwing his wife in *his* bed.

He managed to force himself not to go up the steps into *his* house, retaining enough sense to stumble back to the truck, trying to get his anger under control.

Nearly two hours later, the dude left the house. He wasn't carrying the bottle now and he took his time sauntering along the street as if he didn't have a care in the goddamn world. And what the hell was he anyway, like some thirty-second man, in and out and out the door again in under two hours?

What the hell.

The dude got into his BMW. Doyle got out of the truck and grabbed the tire iron he kept in the back and threw it into the passenger side as the BMW drove off.

Doyle squeezed back in the truck and started the engine. He pulled into the street after the BMW.

22

The dude who screwed his wife—the DWSHW, as Doyle now referred to him—drove west from Georgetown, taking back roads through darkened countryside.

Doyle stayed well back, keeping the BMW's taillights in sight, wondering where the hell this guy was going at this time of night, wondering what he was doing following the guy, maintaining his anger level at a low boil so he could raise it back to rage as needed.

The road twisted and then climbed steeply. Ahead, the taillights disappeared. When Doyle reached the hilltop, he saw the BMW below, turning into a drive that led through trees to an impressive-looking house.

What was the dude doing out here, and why would anyone buy a house in the middle of nowhere? He pulled over to the shoulder and then grabbed the tire iron off the passenger seat and got out of the truck.

He hurried along the gravel road shoulder to the drive. Keeping to the cover provided by the nearby trees, he made his way to the house. A light burned on the ground floor but otherwise the place was in darkness. Doyle could hear music from inside. The DWSHW was in there with someone.

Circling around to the back of the house, Doyle encountered a pressure-treated wood fence. He moved along until he reached a built-in gate. To his surprise, when he lifted the latch, it swung open. He stepped through and found himself facing a good-sized swimming pool. Nearby was a small pool house. Doyle hugged against the side of the pool house, facing sliding doors across the pool. The music was louder now. Barry White? Yeah, that was it. Someone was in there playing Barry goddamn White.

Presently, there was movement from inside, and one of the doors opened. The DWSHW stepped into view, naked, holding a wine glass. "I'm going into the pool," he called back.

The DWSHW perched on the pool's edge, put down his glass and slipped into the water. He floated across the pool and then turned as a second figure came out of the house. A woman, also naked, quite curvy, Doyle noted, also with a drink.

"Come on in," the DWSHW called.

"I'm still pissed at you, Peter," the woman said. She sat at the edge of the pool with her long legs in the water.

Peter. So that was the bastard's name, Doyle thought. A jerk's name. The name of an asshole. *Peter.* Peter the Prick.

"It'll be fine," Peter said, floating over to the woman. "We just have to be patient, that's all."

"Have you even told Marla?" the woman asked.

Marla? Doyle thought. Who is Marla?

"I'm going to talk to her."

"You said you would talk to her." The woman sounded angrier.

"I said I would *try* to talk to her."

The woman pulled her legs out of the water and rose to her feet, body tense. "You bastard. You arrive here, screw the hell out of me, jump into my swimming pool and start making excuses. Well, to hell with you."

She turned and marched away, disappearing back into the house, leaving Peter calling after her: "Karen…come on, Karen."

Okay, Doyle thought, in addition to screwing his wife, this Peter Prick was also having it off with the naked Karen, promising to dump his wife, whose name apparently was Marla. What an asshole, Doyle thought. Peter Prick allowed himself to drift back across the pool, so that his head bobbed around, feet away from where Doyle crouched.

He took a breath and stepped from the pool house. Peter Prick heard Doyle's approach and twisted his head around.

"Hey, Peter," Doyle said, raising the tire iron.

"What are you doing, man?" Peter Prick demanded.

Man? This asshole was calling him *man?* The anger bubbled inside him.

An expression of alarm crossed Peter Prick's face. He opened his mouth to cry out, but Doyle cut off his scream, smashing the tire iron into his head.

A spray of blood flew into the night air.

———

Doyle ran up the drive away from the house hearing with satisfaction a woman's distant, high-pitched scream.

Reaching his truck, he hopped inside and started away. As he drove, he called Daye. To his pleased surprise she answered. "You bitch," he said. "I know what you're up to."

"Doyle, you're not supposed to call me." There was an edge of fear to Daye's voice that Doyle liked. "They've told you time and time again to stay away from me."

"What? So you can screw every prick in town? You're a goddamn slut."

"Doyle, I'm not going to listen to this. I'm hanging up."

"Incidentally, you're not the only slut Peter Prick is screwing. You know that, don't you?"

"Doyle, stop."

"He's married, screwing you, and getting it off with Karen. Hot Karen. She thinks Peter's gonna marry her. But we both know that's bullshit, don't we Daye?"

"I don't know what you're talking about," Daye said in a dull voice.

"Yes, you do. Peter Prick."

Daye started to cry, desperate tears, Doyle thought. "Please, please," she pleaded. "Please leave me alone."

"You're a whore."

"Stop—"

"You're a dead whore—"

The line went dead.

To hell with her, Doyle thought. He'd taken care of Peter Prick.

He'd take care of her soon enough.

23

Jean sat on the edge of her deck, eyes on the garden—her overgrown, half dead, hope-the-neighbors-don't-see-it garden. Otis came and sat on his haunches beside her. She rubbed at his chest. He turned his head slightly, his way of letting her know he appreciated this. Or at least she figured it was his way of letting her know.

"For your information, Otis, I should never have been allowed to buy a house with a garden," she said to the dog. "There should be some sort of bylaw that prevents someone like me from having a garden. I am a garden killer." She stroked his chest some more. "Of course, it would help if I would actually spend some time *working* in the garden."

When she stopped massaging his chest, Otis lay down beside her. Her cellphone began to make sounds. She heaved a silent sigh of relief: an excuse to ignore the garden. She put the phone on speaker and a voice said, "Jean, it's Daye Parker calling."

"Hey," Jean said. "Is everything all right?"

"I didn't want to call you, I thought I could handle this myself," Daye said, her voice breaking.

"It's all right, Daye. What's wrong? What's happened?"

"What else? Doyle happened." Her voice had leveled somewhat. "He called to tell me I was a whore, a dead whore. I'm scared."

"I don't blame you."

"There's a...there's a guy I've been seeing. Last night someone beat him badly, nearly killed him. He's in a coma in hospital."

"And you think Doyle did this?"

"I *know*. I know what he's capable of. Jean, I'm really scared."

"Okay, I'm coming up," Jean said. "Pack a bag and be ready to go when I get there."

"All right," she said in a thin voice.

"In the meantime, keep your doors locked. If he shows up, don't hesitate. Call 911."

"Thank you, Jean."

Jean went upstairs. The lockbox containing her Glock pistol was on a shelf in the closet beside her shoulder holster rig. She eased into the shoulder harness and then worked the combination lock, opened the lid and removed the pistol. She shoved it into the holster, ensuring it was comfortable under her arm and then shrugged into a leather jacket.

Otis was waiting by the door when she came back downstairs. Was she imagining things or was that a look of disapproval? A suggestion he didn't like her leaving the house with a gun?

"Sorry, fella," she said, ruffling her ears. "But sometimes a lady can't be too careful."

Otis cocked his head.

Doubtfully?

———————

Twenty minutes later, Jean parked in front of Daye's darkened house.

Daye was waiting just inside the door, trembling beside an overnight bag. She embraced Jean.

Jean took her bag and together they went out, Daye locking the door behind her. Only when they were back on the highway headed away from town did Daye seem to relax. She reached over and squeezed Jean's arm. "You have no idea how much I appreciate this, Jean."

"You can stay at my place until we figure out what to do," Jean said, keeping her eyes on the dark road ahead. "How do you feel about getting the police involved?"

Daye vehemently shook her head. "The police won't do anything until I'm dead. Besides, there's something weird going on there."

"What do you mean?"

"It sounds crazy, but I think Doyle is somehow being protected by the cops."

"The Halton police?"

"I don't think it's them," Daye said. "Doyle said something about the people you used to work for. The Mounties."

Jean gave her a sidewise glance. "What did Doyle say?"

"That there wasn't much I could do, because the Mounties would make sure nothing happened to him. And a couple of times when we were together, this guy who wasn't supposed to look like a cop but looked like a cop, pulled up in one of those cars that isn't supposed to look like a cop car but is. When I asked Doyle about it, he gave me one of those weird smiles of his and said the less I knew about what was going on, the better it was for me."

24

The two Toronto detectives said they would meet Mickey Dann and Glen Petrusiak inside the Starbucks on Milton's Main Street at 11 a.m. They were right on time, Mickey noted, a good sign. Detective Sergeant Dash Jessup was a heavyset, round-faced woman with frizzy blond hair and eyes like hard emeralds; eyes that Mickey surmised had seen a few things in their time and had adjusted accordingly.

The other detective, Bing Farley, Mickey vaguely remembered from his days at Toronto homicide as the poster boy for the old-fashioned, hard-drinking, chain-smoking cop. Two veterans, the types they would put on a case like the death of Jason Tremblay.

"What are you calling this?" Mickey asked after the four of them had settled with their lattes—for Dash and Mickey—and black coffees for the hard asses, Petrusiak and Farley.

"At the moment, a suspicious death," Dash allowed.

"But?"

"But there is a lot of questionable shit," Dash went on. "Stuff that looks one way, but then looks as though it was arranged that way, and really isn't that way at all."

Dash Jessup leaned forward lowering her voice. "How is it a suspected German sex trafficker ended up shot to death in the house of a former government minister we found dead upstairs in his shower?"

"This is Karl Bauer," Mickey said.

Dash said, "Karl grew up in the eastern sector of Berlin after the wall came down, got involved in the human trafficking business and ended up in jail over there. When he was released in 2016, he somehow got into Canada despite his record."

"He's kept his nose clean here," Mickey said. "Drove a truck at one of the local quarries."

"Well, maybe not that clean," Dash countered. "The Mounties questioned him and a guy named Doyle Parker a year ago when they were investigating possible human trafficking in this region. Supposedly, they were looking into Karl's immigration status, but it doesn't appear as though anything came of that."

"What do you think?" asked Petrusiak. "Did Karl kill Jason Tremblay?"

"That's what we initially suspected," Bing Farley said. "But the autopsy shows Tremblay died of a heart attack."

"You mentioned Doyle Parker," Mickey said. "You know him?"

"His name came up recently in connection with something else. He's got a record. Couple of assault and drug charges. An early possession with intent to distribute stuck, but the others disappeared.

"Okay, there's a dead member of parliament upstairs who died of a heart attack," Mickey said. "Downstairs there's a suspected sex trafficker dead from a gunshot wound."

"That's right," Dash agreed.

Mickey continued, "On the surface it would appear as though, Karl Bauer broke into the house, Jason Trembley confronted him, shot him, then went upstairs, got into the shower and died of a heart attack."

"On the surface," Dash agreed.

"But?"

"For one thing, there was no sign of a murder weapon," Bing Farley said.

"Tremblay had a permit for a handgun but we couldn't find it in the house," Dash said. "Even if by some stretch of the imagination, Tremblay did shoot the guy, why does he then go upstairs and take a shower? Why doesn't he immediately call the police?"

"Not to mention somehow getting rid of the gun," Bing said.

"Maybe he was trying to cover up the shooting," Petrusiak said. "He got rid of the gun, went upstairs, stepped into the shower before dealing with Karl's body and suffered the heart attack that killed him."

The silence that followed suggested no one was buying that theory.

"There's something else," Dash said. "A neighbor of Mr. Tremblay's told officers that she saw a woman go into his house. It turns out that our late, very important Mr. Tremblay, likes ladies who, for a price, drop by."

"She's a young woman named Adara Dunia," Bing said. "Goes by the name Maitland. Strictly high-end. A favorite of Mr. Tremblay's."

"She says she went to his house but couldn't get in and left," Dash said. "But we wonder about that."

"We wonder about a lot of things," Bing Farley added.

"Except you know Karl Bauer was involved in the sex trade," Mickey offered. "It sounds like this guy Tremblay was a regular participant in that trade. Maybe he received a visit from one of his women. Karl delivered her. Maybe something went wrong and when Karl came around to straighten it out, he got shot. Could be the gun is missing because the woman who shot him took it with her when she disappeared."

"That's a theory all right," Dash Jessup agreed. "But still …" She allowed her voice to trail off.

"How can we help, detectives?" Petrusiak filled the silence that had ensued.

"Karl's employer," Farley said. "A quarry around here?"

"Halton Rock Quarry. Just outside Georgetown," Mickey said. "We can drive up there with you."

"Much appreciated," Dash said.

"There's one other thing," Mickey said.

"What's that?"

"Doyle Parker. He works at the same quarry. Couple of reasons why I'd like to talk to him, too."

"Then let's do it," Dash said.

25

The sign at the edge of the roadway leading to the Halton Rock Quarry advised visitors to check in at the gate before venturing further. Except there was no one at the gate, a single barrier that would rise with the correct code pressed into the keypad.

Instead, Petrusiak was able to ease the unmarked SUV in which the four detectives were travelling onto the shoulder around the gate and then proceed along a twisting road past a mountain of crushed rock to a parking area.

An aluminum-side office trailer stood nearby. Beyond, beneath a threatening sky, the gray cliffsides of the quarry. Trucks were parked in a line adjacent to the quarry not far from iron monster-like machinery ready to pounce.

It was unnaturally quiet as the detectives trailed across to the trailer. Nobody appeared to be working today. Mickey stopped and turned to the others. "Glen, why don't you and Bing stay out here and have a look around while Dash and I have a word with whoever's inside?"

It was obvious Petrusiak didn't like that idea. He started to say something and then thought better of it. He nodded and said, "We'll take a look around."

Mickey followed Dash up the steps. She pounded on the steel door. A voice said, "Yeah, come on in."

Dash opened the door allowing Mickey to enter first. An old man in a recliner jerked to attention near one of the two office desks. A woman in jeans and a pullover working at a laptop on the second desk, removed a cigarette from her mouth, suspicion crowding a lined face showing the ravages of age and a lifetime of smoking.

"What can I do for you folks?" the woman asked in a raspy smoker's voice, and not a friendly one, Mickey decided.

Mickey showed her his identification and Dash did as well. "I'm Detective Mickey Dann from the Halton Police." He indicated Dash. "Dash Jessup is with the Metropolitan Toronto Police."

The old man shifted uneasily in his chair, narrowing his eyes as though to get a better look at the intruders. "You'll have to excuse us," he said, once he had satisfied himself. "We don't get a lot of visitors out here. Surprised they didn't phone from security."

"There was no security when we came in," Mickey said.

"You entered by the wrong gate," the woman said in an accusatory voice.

"Sorry about that," Mickey said. He looked at the old man. "Would you like to identify yourselves?"

"Wouldn't like to particularly," the old man said with a smile, "but we certainly can do it, if that's what the law requires. I'm Wilbur Shirley, but everyone calls me Dad. This here is my wife, Gail." He added with a chuckle, "Everyone calls her Gail."

"You the managers here?" Dash asked.

"Owners and managers," Dad Shirley asserted. "For your information this is one of the last privately owned quarries in the province. The rest, big international conglomerates operating around here, raping the land you ask me. This one's just about played out now, but we're making the best of the situation, pulling what rock we can out."

"Looks like there's plenty of rock around here," Mickey said.

"That there is," Dad Shirley acknowledged. "Trouble is, government only allows us to go so deep, then we hit a water table."

"We wanted to ask you about one of your employees," Dash Jessup interjected.

"Yeah? Which one would that be?"

"Karl Bauer."

Dad frowned. "Karl don't work here any longer."

"You know he's dead," Dash said.

"Heard something on the news," Dad said noncommittally.

"How long did Karl work here?"

"I dunno," Dad shrugged. "Not long." He looked over at his wife. "What about it, dear? How long Karl work here?"

"About three years, as I recall," Gail stated.

"What did he do around here?" Mickey asked.

"Drove a truck," came Dad's prompt reply.

"Did you know Karl had a criminal record?"

"Didn't know, didn't need to know," Dad snapped. "Can a fella handle a truck and show up on time? That's all that interests me. Karl did both."

"When did he leave?"

"Honey?" Dad was looking at Gail again.

She shrugged. "I guess a couple of weeks ago."

"He left? Or you fired him?"

"A little of both, I'd say."

"Which is it?" Dash demanded.

"Well, let's say he quit before we could fire him. How's that?"

"Why were you going to fire him?"

"Same reason we fire most fellas. Karl didn't show up when he was supposed to."

"You just said he did show up."

"He showed up till he didn't. Then he quit. End of story."

"Any idea how he would end up shot to death in a Toronto house?"

"The end of the sad saga of Karl Bauer, I guess," Dad said. "Can't say much more than that."

"What about Doyle Parker?" Mickey asked.

Dad hesitated a little longer than he should have before he asked, "What about him?"

"Doyle works here, does he not?"

Dad and Gail traded glances. "He does," Dad said slowly, as though not quite sure of his answer.

"What does he do?"

"Drives a truck," Dad replied with the same speed he had addressed a description of Karl Bauer's job.

Mickey couldn't help but smile. "Everybody drives a truck, it seems."

"We need truck drivers. Doyle is one of them."

"We'd like to talk to him," Mickey said.

Dad looked over at his wife. Gail paused before she said, "Doyle's got the day off."

"Karl Bauer was fired. Doyle Parker has the day off. Who's out there driving the trucks?"

"If you're looking for a job..." Dad said, grinning.

"Maybe you could give us an address for Doyle," Mickey said.

"Don't have an address," Gail said promptly.

"You don't keep addresses for your employees?"

"People come, they go," Gail said. "It's a pretty transient business. Doesn't make sense to keep a lot of records."

"What about a phone number, then?"

"Let me see if I have his number," Gail said.

26

"You sure you know where this place is?" Maitland asked. She was steering the rented Ford Transit van along country roads somewhere outside Georgetown.

Shanifa in response to the question—not the first time it had been asked—merely pointed ahead, stating, "the next intersection, turn left."

Maitland gave her a look, but then they were approaching a Something Sideroad so she swung right onto a gravel roadway that quickly rose to the crest of a hill.

"You're not even sure they'll come," Maitland managed to say, fighting with the wheel of the van.

"They will come," Shanifa replied confidently.

"And no one's watching them?"

"Karl was. But not anymore."

"If that's the case, if no one's watching them, why haven't they run away?"

"Because they are frightened and there is no place to go."

"Then what's going to change?"

"They no longer have to be frightened. There is a place to go."

When Maitland reached the crest, she could see in the shallow valley below, a pair of ramshackle log cottages near a lake.

"This is it?" Maitland asked.

Shanifa nodded.

Maitland turned onto a track running to one of the cottages. "Park anywhere along here," Shanifa ordered. As Maitland came to a stop, Shanifa had her handbag in her lap and was pulling out the Beretta. She looked up and saw the unhappy grimace on Maitland's face. "Just in case," Shanifa said.

She stuck the gun in her belt and got out. Maitland gave a groan of resignation before following her.

Two rusted bikes were collapsed against the log wall next to a broken-down Muskoka chair. Shanifa opened a ratty screen door and entered a cramped sitting room, the air musty and thick with the smell of marijuana. Two young women sprawled on a pair of sagging couches. Two more were on the two double beds. A fifth woman was entering from the other room.

Any thoughts Maitland might have had about a jubilant greeting for the returning Shanifa were quickly disabused as the women, casual in tights and T-shirts, stared at the new arrivals with lifeless, disinterested eyes. It struck Maitland that everyone was doped to the eyeballs.

"Greetings, Amber," Shanifa said to the tiny, voluptuous woman who had just come into view.

Amber blinked in surprise. "What are you doing here?" she asked.

"I have come for you." Shanifa pointed to the tall, lanky woman on the bed. "And you Nataliya."

"Me? What do you want with me?"

"And Daria," Shanifa said, indicating the heavyset woman with purple hair. "Kiva and Bora. All of you."

Daria shrugged non-committally. "I hear you ran away, Shanifa. Why are you crazy enough to come back?"

"There is a van outside," Shanifa announced. "Collect your things and come with me."

Amber regarded Shanifa with slack-jawed ambivalence. "Why? Why would we go anywhere with you?"

Shanifa thrust her hand in Maitland's direction. "My friend Maitland and I have started a new business. We want all of you to be part of our business."

"What kind of business?" demanded Amber.

"A business in which you are no longer slaves. A business where, if you want to work, you get paid for it. You don't want to, okay. No one beats you or rapes you. No one threatens."

Daria shook her head in disbelief. "You taking us to heaven, Shanifa? Is that what you're promising?"

"Out of this hell, that's for sure," Shanifa answered.

Amber said, "What about Karl? The Shirleys? How are you going to protect us?"

"Karl is dead," Shanifa said. "He will not bother anyone again. I will protect you from the Shirleys."

"How can you protect us?" Nataliya sounded disdainful.

Shanifa drew the gun out and held it high in the air. Everyone's attention was riveted on her.

"If the Shirleys come for you, they will know the business end of this gun, the same way Karl did," she announced in the sort of strong, authoritative voice that took Maitland by surprise. "Collect your things. I am taking you to the promised land."

Twenty minutes later, the five women had gathered up their meagre belongings. They had also prepared the vinyl zippered wardrobe bags containing their 'costumes,' the sexy working clothes they wore for the whales. Maitland took one look and decided they were cheap and awful.

"We've got to get rid of this crap," Maitland said.

"First we need income," Shanifa said.

"I can get us some seed money," Maitland said.

Shanifa looked at her. "I don't like too many people knowing of our business."

"This guy is discrete, don't worry. Let me take care of it."

The same guy Maitland made her secretive phone calls to? Shanifa wondered.

Once the wardrobe bags and the luggage were stowed into the van, Shanifa disappeared and came back lugging two polyethylene gas cans. She handed one of the cans to a surprised Maitland. "Empty the can on the sofas and floor," Shanifa ordered. "I'll take care of the bedrooms."

"What are you doing?"

"Just do it," Shanifa said.

Reluctantly, Maitland undid the plastic cap and went over to one of the sofas and began splashing the gasoline over it. Then she splashed more gas around the room. Shanifa came back, took one look at what Maitland was doing, and grabbed the can from her. She energetically finished pouring the gas on the floor and walls, spilling it along the short corridor to the kitchen.

The rank smell of gasoline filled the air. Shanifa threw the can down and ordered Maitland outside.

The women had gathered at the van, staring expectantly as Maitland emerged from the cabin. She joined the group. No one said anything. From inside the cabin came a short sharp woosh as the gasoline caught fire. Soon smoke began to pour out the open doorway. Maitland was just starting to worry when Shanifa emerged ahead of flames bursting through the interior.

Fire crackled and consumed the cabin's dry logs and timbers, black smoke rising into the air, the women applauding and cheering. The cabin's roof exploded. Maitland was amazed at the fire's speed.

The five young women congregated around Shanifa, looking at her in a new way. A worshipful way.

Maitland wondered fleetingly if she wasn't watching a heroine being born; the Joan of Arc of whores.

27

A chilly gray morning, Jean awakening, Otis's fine head up in anticipation of another day with his pal.

Daye remained asleep in the guest bedroom as Jean came downstairs, Otis eagerly leading the way. According to the kitchen clock it was 7:30. She was pleasantly surprised that she had actually slept in.

She fed Otis his morning kibble which he dived into with his customary eagerness, seeming to forgive its late arrival. She busied herself making coffee, hoping that Daye would be okay with the hazelnut flavor that she preferred, having decided long ago that the less coffee tasted like coffee, the better.

Once her machine finished emitting the groans and gurgles signifying it was on life support, she poured coffee into a mug and added lots of milk. With coffee in hand, she sat at the kitchen table, trying to wake up. Otis finished his kibble and then padded over to her. He sat on his haunches, cocked his head and regarded her expectantly. The joys of having a big dog. No matter how you felt, they always demanded their morning run and no excuses.

"Sorry, pal," she said, addressing the dog, "I'm feeling lazy. Give me a chance to finish my coffee."

Otis gave a wag of his fine tail but did not move from his perch beside her chair. Her cellphone made noises.

"It's the guy with the shitty truck."

"Jim Callahan," she said.

"I wasn't sure you'd remember," Jim said.

"A guy driving a truck, fighting for a better world, how could I forget?"

"Why I hang onto the truck. Makes me unforgettable."

"How goes the fight?"

"Stopping quarries is a slow business, I'm learning. What about you? Why haven't you called?"

"Was I supposed to?"

"Not necessarily, although I have been waiting by the phone and hoping."

"I've been busy," Jean said. "How's that for an excuse?" No lie, she thought to herself. In fact, she'd almost forgotten her encounter with him.

"I couldn't wait any longer, so here I am calling you."

"I'm glad you called," she said.

"That's a relief," Jim said. "I thought I'd see if I could talk you into coming on one of my trail breaks."

Jean thought that the last thing she needed was to go traipsing through the wilds of Georgetown. She had enough to deal with. Aloud she said, "I'd love to do that, Jim. But this is not a good time."

"No? I'm crushed."

"Can I get a rain check?"

"That's a phrase I haven't heard for a while."

"I probably haven't used it since I was a teenager," she admitted.

"When all the boys were after you," Jim said.

"Well, I wouldn't go *that* far."

"Tell you what," Jim said. "When things settle down in your life, why don't you give me a call? The trails will still be there."

"I'd like that," Jean said, wondering if she really would like it.

After she hung up, she thought some more about Jim. Did she really want in her life some guy in a pickup truck, hiking nature trails, pointing out favorite bushes and birds? That is if Jim Callahan *had* favorite bushes and birds. She had trouble imagining that scenario unfolding with much success. Wilderness guys in pickup trucks were not her style, raising the question of what exactly was her style. Middle-age cops who couldn't give a shit about her? Yes, that was more like it.

She was a softie for Otis. For men in pickup trucks? "I'm not so sure," she said to Otis. "I think I'll stick with you, puppy dog. All you require is kibble, a walk, and lots of pets. Men are a whole lot more complicated, let me tell you."

"Are you talking to your dog?" Daye came into view, clad in the shorts and the T-shirt Jean had lent her the night before.

"Doesn't everyone?"

"I don't know," Daye said, eyeing Otis hesitantly. "I don't know anything about dogs."

"They make you a better person," Jean said.

"Ah, that explains it," Daye said, seating herself on the other side of the table, away from Otis who kept his gaze expectantly on Jean.

"Would you like some coffee?" Jean asked.

"I can get it," Daye said.

"No, it's okay. Stay put." Jean rose to withdraw a mug from the cupboard and pour coffee. "What do you take? Milk?"

"Lots of milk, please," Daye said.

Jean returned and placed the cup in front of Daye. "Thanks," she said. "I really appreciate—well, everything. You know. Taking me in like this."

"Hey, you're family," Jean replied.

"Well, sort of, I guess."

"What about something to eat? Are you hungry?"

Daye shrugged. "I guess so, yeah. Sure."

Jean made her some toast while Otis looked on with a mixture of attentiveness and—if Jean was correctly reading his mood—disappointment at not yet getting his walk.

Jean poured more coffee for herself as Daye spread marmalade on her toast. She waited until Daye had finished devouring the toast—and that's what it was, devouring—before she said, "We should talk about Doyle."

The color drained from Daye's face. "Right now, I don't even want to think about him, let alone talk."

"I don't blame you," Jean said. "But we need to come up with a strategy for dealing with him."

"Strategy?" Daye sounded as though she had never before heard the word.

"So that he doesn't threaten you anymore."

"I don't know how we do that," Daye said. "Unless you kill him," she added.

"On the way here, you told me he was working with the RCMP."

"Yeah, well, I don't know for sure, but if it's true, that just makes him more confident he can get away with anything."

"Yes, but why would the RCMP be interested in him in the first place? Why would they want to protect a low-level creep like Doyle?"

Daye shrugged.

"They wouldn't be interested in him if he didn't know something they want to know."

Daye thought about this for a time and then said, "He used to talk about running errands for the people he worked for."

"The Shirleys?"

"They're the people who own Halton Rock Quarry," Daye said.

"I know who they are. What did he do for them other than drive a truck?"

"He'd pick stuff up for them at a cabin not far from the quarry. When we were first married, he would disappear and I was pretty sure he was seeing someone else. One night I followed him. He drove to this cabin."

"What did he do there?"

"He unloaded cases of bottled water and then left."

"Was anyone else there?"

"A big guy. I think his name was Karl. Karl and a couple of teenagers."

"Karl worked at the quarry, too?"

"Yeah, I guess so. Doyle didn't like him much, if I remember correctly."

"What about the teenagers. Any idea why they were there?"

"I guess they were with Karl, I don't know. I never thought much about it after everything started to go to shit. By then I wished he would have an affair so he would stay away from me."

"You say a cabin. What kind of cabin?"

"I don't know, a cabin built of logs. A cottage, I guess."

"Do you think you could find this place again?"

"I suppose so. Why?"

"I'd like to drive out there," Jean said.

"Drive out there?" Daye looked surprised.

"And take a look around."

28

They reached Georgetown in the early afternoon, and then, guided by a surprisingly accurate Daye, drove west and then north along country roads passing prosperous-looking horse farms stocked with sleek mares and stallions grazing in meadows of undulating green, contrasting with ranks of spanking-new bungalows and townhouses, evidence of the encroaching urban sprawl moving resolutely west and north from Toronto.

"Turn right at the next crossing," Daye ordered. And as soon as Jean did, the road began to climb a steep hill and that's when they both saw the plume of smoke, a smudge against the pale sky.

"What's that?" Jean asked.

Daye, confused, shook her head, not saying anything. At the hilltop the road plunged into a narrow valley not far from a small lake surrounded by forest. As they came over the crest it was immediately apparent what was producing the smoke—the smoldering ruin of what appeared to have been a cottage.

"Is that it?" Jean asked.

"That *was* it," Daye amended.

The two women got out to survey the damage. Below, Jean could see a dirt track leading off to the blackened remains of the cabin. A second nearby cabin looked untouched. "What do you suppose happened?" Daye asked.

"A fire," Jean said, stating the obvious. "The question is what caused it? Was this an accident? Or did someone torch the place?"

Jean was distracted by movement near the untouched cabin. Two figures emerged, a tall, bespectacled Asian man clad in black and a short, squat woman in baggy jeans and an equally baggy pullover. How long had it been since she had combed that tangled bush of hair framing her red face?

"Any idea who they are?" Jean asked.

Daye stepped forward, squinting to get a better view, and then shook her head. "No idea," she said.

The two figures moved to the edge of the ruins. The Asian man stepped over charred beams. From what Jean could see, he didn't look happy. The woman fished a pack of cigarettes from her pocket. The Asian man turned and said something to the woman. She put the cigarettes away.

Whoever these two were, the Asian man was calling the shots, Jean decided.

Presently, the two walked away, the Asian man moving briskly, the fat woman hurrying to catch up.

"Get in the car," Jean said.

Daye looked even more worried. "What are you going to do?"

"I'll come right back," Jean said.

She scrambled down the hillside to the valley floor, hurrying around the burned-out cabin, reaching the woods into which the Asian man and the heavyset woman had disappeared. Spikey buckthorn trees closed in as she made her way along a narrow track.

The sky darkened in concert with a bitter rising wind, making Jean shiver as she emerged from the stand of buckthorns and passed two abandoned red vans slumped at odd angles. The land dipped onto a flat plain stretching to a body of water framed by high, broken cliffs. Jean realized with a start that this was the Hidden Quarry where the bodies of three young woman had been discovered. She was now seeing it from a different vantage point.

Halfway across the plain, stood a shed where Jean could see the Asian man talking to the fat woman.

The woman gesticulated with her hands, trying to explain something to the unmoving Asian man. The heavyset woman threw up her hands and then stopped abruptly, peering into the trees where Jean crouched. She immediately drew back.

Too late.

The fat woman had seen her.

"I thought I saw something," Gail Shirley said.

Cai Mak turned and followed Gail's gaze into the woods. "There's nothing," he said, dismissively.

"There was something," Gail insisted.

"Getting paranoid isn't going to help," Cai Mak said irritably.

"I'm not paranoid, I'm careful," Gail said.

"No, you're not," Cai snapped. "You and that fool you're married to, you're careless. You left product unattended. My product, incidentally. The product I entrusted to you. Now it's missing and for good measure before they disappeared, they burned down your cabin."

"It could have been an accident," Gail said.

"I can smell the gasoline from here," Cai said. "Those bitches torched the place."

"I'll take care of this," Gail said, trying to sound much more confident than she felt. "We'll get the product back."

"And what about the shit that went down in Rosedale?"

"Look, I know there are problems—"

"Problems?" Cai Mak said in an astonished voice. "What's her name?"

"Shanifa," Gail said.

"More missing product. Not to mention a dead whale and one of your employees shot to death."

"Like I explained before, we suspect Shanifa."

"Yeah, this kid from Africa caused the whale to have a heart attack and then somehow got her hands on a gun and used it to murder your guy."

"In fact, that's how we believe it happened. The police have said nothing about any young woman, so it stands to reason Karl tried to stop her and she shot him and then disappeared."

Cai gave her a long hard look. "Get those women back," he said.

"We'll make it happen, don't worry," Gail said.

He swept away from her, walking briskly, a man on a mission, Gail thought, a man you don't want to screw with.

As soon as he was out of sight, Gail stuck a cigarette in her mouth and then turned away from the wind, trying to light it. When that was finally accomplished, she took a long, satisfying draw on the cigarette.

She blew a plume of smoke into the air and said aloud, "Jesus."

29

By the time Doyle Parker reached Georgetown and parked down the street from his wife's house, the dark mass of anger he could summon at a moment's notice had grown red hot. He could kill someone; someone like his bitch wife. He marched along the street to the house. It stood in darkness. No sign of anyone home. Of course. He paused by the gate, angry disappointment washing over him. The bitch must have taken off. But where? Where would she go?

"Hey, Doyle."

Doyle swung around as two figures came out of the darkness. A man and a woman.

The man flashed identification in Doyle's face. "Halton Police. I'm Mickey Dann. This is Detective Sergeant Dash Jessup from the Metropolitan Police Service."

Doyle could only stare, his mind a blur. What the goddamn hell?

"Have you got a moment to answer a few questions, Doyle?" asked the woman named Dash Jessup.

"What's this about?" Doyle demanded, hoping these two couldn't hear the thumping of his heart.

"We've got a car just down the street," Mickey said. "Why don't we sit in there? More comfortable than standing on the street."

"I'm fine right here," Mickey said.

"Doyle, get in the car." Dash Jessup's tone didn't encourage a debate.

Doyle followed the two detectives along the block to where a nondescript brown sedan was parked. Doyle kicked himself for being so fixated on Daye that he missed what now looked like the cliché of an unmarked cop car.

Damn that bitch, anyway.

Doyle crouched in the back with the cop named Mickey Dann, while the Jessup woman slid into the front seat and then twisted around so that she faced Doyle. Everyone was cast in a half light from the street.

Mickey addressed Doyle. "Tell us what you know about Karl Bauer."

For a moment, the name didn't register. And then it hit him. Right, Karl. Asking about him was the last thing Doyle had been expecting.

"Doyle," Dash Jessup chimed in. "Answer the question."

"I don't know anyone named Karl," Doyle said.

"Karl Bauer," Mickey repeated. "You don't know Karl Bauer?"

"How should I know him?"

"He worked at the same quarry you do," Dash said. "You work with a guy and you don't know his name?"

"Oh, yeah," Doyle heard himself amending. "The Kraut. That's how I know him. At the quarry. I don't usually hear his real name. The Kraut. Kind of threw me off."

"I'll bet it did," said Mickey dryly.

"I mean, the Kraut, I don't know. He works at the quarry. I nod to him when I see him. That's as far as it goes. The Kraut. I don't know anything about him."

"When was the last time you saw him?"

"I don't know," Doyle said. "Today at work, I guess. I don't know."

"Today at work," Jessup said.

"I guess," Doyle answered.

"It would have been hard for you to see him today," Mickey said.

"Yeah? Why is that?"

"Karl's dead," Mickey said.

"Okay, I guess I must have been mistaken."

"You don't seem surprised that he's dead," Dash said.

"Like I said, I hardly knew the guy."

"You hardly knew him."

"Like I said."

"Okay, supposing I told you we believe the late Karl Bauer was mixed up in human trafficking in the area, and that you are involved too."

"That's bullshit," Doyle said. He made himself sound appalled at the idea.

"Is it?" Dash said. "Then why did the RCMP question the two of you a year ago?"

"They got bad information," Doyle snapped.

"You and Karl, the guy you hardly know," Mickey said.

"Talk to the Mounties, they know me," Doyle said with unexpected confidence.

"What? They're going to tell us you're not mixed up in sex trafficking?" Mickey said.

"Sex trafficking? What is that? You have sex in the traffic? Man, I've had sex everywhere, but never in traffic."

"Okay, Doyle, you're an innocent friend of the Mounties. Tell us what you're doing out here tonight."

"What do you mean, what am I doing?"

"I've had a complaint about you," Mickey continued.

"Why would anyone complain about me?"

"Your wife," Mickey said. "She might complain about you, don't you think?"

"A misunderstanding," Doyle said.

"What? She misunderstood when you beat her up?"

"I never beat her up," Doyle maintained.

"She's lying?"

"We're working on our issues. It's a matter to time before we get back together."

"Bad information. Misunderstandings. False accusations." Dash Jessup leaned across the seat for a closer look at Doyle. "You're pretty hard done by, aren't you?"

"Yeah, people are out to get me," Doyle agreed.

"You've been ordered several times to stay away from your wife," Dash pointed out.

"That's old news," Doyle said. "Daye's gonna have that order taken away."

"But right now it stands," Mickey said. "What are you doing in front of her house?"

"I was worried about her," Doyle said.

"You're not supposed to worry about her," Mickey said. "You're supposed to stay away from her."

"That's all going to change," Doyle insisted. "We're going to—what's the word?—reconcile, that's it."

Mickey leaned close to Doyle, grabbing his jacket. "Listen, you asshole, you're a goddamn wifebeater and liar. I find that you're anywhere near this neighborhood again and I will come for you personally and I guarantee that I will screw up whatever else you're involved in."

"Not involved in anything," Doyle said.

Mickey let go of Doyle and Dash said, "Don't get the idea this is the end of it. As mean as my friend Mickey is, I'm meaner, and I'm coming for you and the other assholes who are involved in this sex trade."

"Get out," Mickey said. "Get the hell out of my sight."

Doyle tried to look cool and unshaken prying himself out the car, like these two hadn't scared the shit out of him. But in the darkness, fumbling for the door latch, finally getting the door open just as he was about to make his cool Steve-McQueen-type exit, Mickey gave him a hard shove sending him sprawling onto the street.

The cops' car sped off as he struggled to his feet, trying to shake off the combination of humiliation and panic he was feeling. He fished into his pocket for his cellphone, then angrily punched out the number they'd given him.

"What is it?" snapped a voice on the other end of the line.

"I'm having trouble with local law enforcement assholes, okay?" Doyle spoke angrily into the phone. "Trouble you said I wouldn't have."

"Tell me what happened," the voice said.

30

Otis waited by the door, ready for his morning walk as Jean came downstairs in her sweats, still half asleep. Upstairs, she could hear Daye's gentle snores, marveling again at how much the young woman could sleep, thinking that this could be the first time in a very long time she had been able to get any rest.

"Of course, Daye doesn't have a young fellow like you, Otis, who demands to be walked every morning," she said, attaching the leash to Otis's collar. For his part, Otis merely cocked his head and jumped to his feet, beating his tail against the wall as Jean opened the door.

Outside, the sun brightened the tree-lined avenue dropping toward Main Street, Otis yanking Jean along, the cliché of the dog walking his human, his powerful muscles straining as they navigated the almost-deserted Main Street, turning onto James, Otis intent on reaching his destination: Rotary Park and the Mill Pond adjacent to the park.

Left or right along the shaded path beside the creek? Otis barreled right, snout to the ground, sniffing out his territory, Jean dragged behind through dappled sunlight, past a couple of fishermen, optimists, Jean thought fleetingly. Otis paused long enough to mark his territory before continuing on to what the locals referred to as the chicken pluckin' place, otherwise known as an abattoir, and then out onto the grassy knoll where a gazebo overlooked the water and a lone figure leaned against the railing.

He called, "Jean."

She brought Otis to a reluctant halt, squinting her eyes, trying to see who lurked in the gazebo's shadows. "Over here, Jean," the figure called, moving just enough so that the early sun caught the side of Inspector Walter Duke's bullet head, accentuating the lines of his equine face. The prairie dog with two pieces of anthracite for eyes, the bastard who had played such an important part in ruining her life as a Mounted Police officer. Not the last person she ever wanted to see again, but close.

She stood with the dog, not wanting to approach him. When he saw that, Walter Duke came off the gazebo, looking trim and professional in a somber gray suit that could not hide the way he carried himself, the authoritative stride signaling he could only be a cop.

"How have you been, Jean?" he asked as he drew closer to her.

"I was doing pretty well until a couple of minutes ago," Jean said. "What are you doing here?"

Otis, realizing his walk was interrupted, settled impatiently, head cocked, closely inspecting this stranger, as though to ascertain friend or foe. No friend, Jean thought.

Duke smiled a smile that was no smile at all, merely the opening and closing of his thin mouth to show unexpected white teeth. "Should I say I was in the neighborhood and thought I'd drop by? Or would it be better to say I thought it time we had a talk."

"There's nothing to talk about," Jean said.

Duke nodded at Otis. "Your dog friendly?"

"He's friendly with friends."

"Then I'd better be careful, hadn't I?" Duke issued another mirthless smile before adding, "Give me a few minutes, Jean. There's a bench over there. We sit, we talk, I fade away into the ether."

"Talk about what?"

"Please, sit."

She hesitated and then nodded. "Since you're in the neighborhood…"

He joined her on the bench with a view of the pond through the trees. Otis was tensed beside Jean, still not quite sure what to make of this stranger. Jean felt the same way.

"Do you mind if I smoke?" Duke asked.

"Yeah, I do," Jean said.

"Okay, no problem." Duke leaned against the back of the bench, trying to make it look as though he was comfortable when he obviously wasn't.

"I'm not sure you're aware of the sex trafficking that's going on in the Halton region."

"I suppose it's a problem everywhere," Jean said.

"This area is growing faster than any other region in Canada, and therefore it's attracted some pretty nasty players," Duke went on. "That's why for the past year or so, in coordination with local law enforcement representatives, including Metro Toronto and Halton police, we've been targeting high-end sex rings."

Duke went on: "We believe what goes on around here is part of a larger organization run out of Toronto, but has its origins in South Korea."

"How has the targeting worked for you?"

Duke grimaced as he said, "Not as we'd hoped, to be frank. We don't have a whole lot to show for our efforts. We need to try something else."

"Okay," Jean said, not sure where Duke was taking this.

"I know you've had your difficulties with us."

"Like being thrown out of the Force in disgrace after my sergeant tried to rape me," Jean interjected. "Like being vilified in the media before I got out there and finally was able to clear my name after almost getting myself killed. Is that what you mean by 'difficulties?'"

"Mistakes were made and I think we've acknowledged those mistakes, Jean, both with a public apology and a substantial cash settlement. I've even urged you to rejoin the Force I believe you still love, despite everything that's happened."

Duke paused to see how Jean reacted to this. When she didn't, he continued: "Cut to the chase. We need someone who can go undercover and infiltrate the organization behind this local sex trafficking. We think this is something you could do for us."

Jean couldn't quite believe what she was hearing. "You've got to be kidding me."

"Sending in a serving officer simply won't work as far as I'm concerned. Too many chances for leaks. But you, Jean, no one would suspect you. A disgraced cop, looking for a new line of work."

"As a prostitute?"

"Not quite. We would set you up as an organizer, someone who knows how to deal with the problems that arise in the sex business."

"How am I supposed to convince anyone of that?" Jean asked. "This isn't something where you can fill out an application and go for an interview."

"We have a confidential informant," Duke said. "He hasn't been much use, but he can get you inside, introduce you to the right people. According to our CI, there have been disruptions lately within the ring. The Toronto bosses are not happy. They are anxious to reorganize. You would be coming in at exactly the right time."

"What makes you think I would ever in a million years do this?"

"Because it's what you do," Duke answered. "An opportunity you can't turn down. I've been following your activities, Jean. You keep saying you're not in the game any longer, but events show that you still are— you can't stay away."

"That's where you're wrong," Jean stood and immediately Otis was on his feet, anxious to resume their walk. "I'm probably lying when I say it's good to see you again, Inspector."

"You probably are," Duke responded.

Jean started off with Otis eagerly leading the way. Duke called after her: "One other thing."

She paused and then turned to him.

"Do this for us, go undercover, see what you can find out about these people, and you can write your own return ticket back to the Force. You get your old job back with a promotion, along with what I think you've been looking for all along."

"What's that, Inspector?"

"Vindication."

Jean gave him a hard look. Duke rose to his feet, returning her gaze, the black-as-coal eyes unblinking.

Daring her.

He handed her a card. "My private number," he said. "In case you change your mind."

Otis tugged impatiently at the leash. Jean allowed him to pull her away.

31

Back at the house, Jean expected to find Daye up and sipping the coffee she had left for her. But the coffee pot was untouched, the house curiously silent.

Just as well, Jean thought. She needed a moment to digest Duke's offer—the offer that, true to form when dealing with the RCMP, wasn't much of an offer at all. Otis was underfoot waiting expectantly so she fed him his morning treat and then poured more coffee for herself.

Of course, she wouldn't have anything to do with Duke. What he was suggesting made no sense. It would be madness on her part to get involved. She was out; she was not about to be pulled back in.

Crazy.

She paused to listen for movement from upstairs. There was none. She called, "Daye, are you awake?"

No answer. Otis was at her side now. He followed Jean up the stairs. She went along the hall to the guest bedroom. The door was open. Jean stepped inside. Well, she thought, at least Daye made the bed. A sheet of lined paper lay on the duvet. It contained a single scrawled word:

Thanks.

Jean snapped suddenly awake in darkness, thinking she had heard something, no idea what time it was, sensing it was well past the midnight hour. Otis stirred contentedly beside her; a good dog in a deep, satisfied sleep. Whatever had awakened her had not moved Otis. Not the keenest watch dog. Or maybe he was, knowing there was nothing to be concerned about. Jean was not convinced. She moved carefully away so as not to disturb him, sitting up in bed, listening.

There was the low, insistent hum of the air conditioning, otherwise, nothing. She lay back on her pillow, wide awake now.

Thinking.

Angry with herself for allowing her mind to fill with the words of Walter Duke. Words she didn't want to hear, didn't want to consider. She thought about Daye, at once angry with her for walking out without a word—well, one word, *thanks*—at the same time worried about her safety, that while she walked Otis, Doyle Parker had somehow convinced her to go away with him.

No, surely that wasn't a possibility.

Still, if she had learned nothing else during her years as a Mountie, anything was possible when it came to screwed-up relationships. She could add a few of her own to that list. Mickey Dann could be on it. Except for the fact you couldn't even call what they had— *have?*—a relationship.

Could you?

Her mind was wandering again. She got out of bed and that woke Otis. He sat up, his eyes blazing with curiosity. "Sorry, boy," she said to him. "Mind all over the place. Can't sleep."

She picked up the phone. She didn't have to look at the card he had given her. She'd looked at the number once and it was forever lodged in her head.

Her stupid, brainless, heedless head.

The phone sounded a dozen times before he picked it up.

"You bastard," Jean said.

"There is that," Inspector Walter Duke said.

"What do I have to do?" Jean demanded.

32

Two of the women, Nataliya and Daria, initially said they didn't want go back to what they previously had been forced into.

Amber, Kiva, and Bora agreed once Maitland outlined the new work arrangements that not only provided salaries, but freed the women of their former obligations and debts.

Maitland and Shanifa would take forty per cent, leaving the women with sixty per cent of their earnings. Using the cash provided by the late Jason Tremblay, Maitland was able to fund the shopping sprees that outfitted the women in the elegant designer clothes that were a far cry from the cheap, shared outfits the Shirleys had provided. This was now a proper high-end business, Maitland announced. The "models" as she referred to the girls, would appear in the elegant clothes that complemented the wealthy individuals whose discretion could be relied upon.

The whales liked the new way of doing things, particularly the absence of thug-like males showing up at the door with the young woman they were supposedly protecting, but who in reality acted more like prison guards. Also, unlike before, if the whale felt more comfortable meeting at a hotel that was fine. It was a much better arrangement all around, good enough to make

Nataliya and Daria change their minds and decide to work.

They were doing well, Shanifa conceded after Maitland expressed frustration at her partner's lack of excitement for their success. However, she went on, there remained a problem—a *big* problem.

"What kind of problem?" Maitland demanded in exasperation.

"The bad people," Shanifa said.

"What bad people?"

"The bad people I ran away from. They are still out there. They will be looking for me and the others."

"How can you be sure?"

"Because they work for even worse people. People in Toronto. They will be looking for me and the others."

"Okay, supposing that is the case. What do you propose we do about it?"

"It must be taken care of," Shanifa asserted.

———

Gail Shirley took a break from the QuickBooks page she had up on her screen and gazed out the window at the full moon crossed with thin clouds above the quarry floor. Jack Jones was softly singing "Once Upon A Time" his mellow voice emitting from the portable sound system she had mounted on a shelf behind her desk.

Yeah, Jack, once upon a time, all right. She liked Jack Jones in his prime, the way the singer's voice soothed her. Yeah, once upon a time. These days, she needed all the soothing she could get.

Gail lit her—what?—fiftieth cigarette of the day, thinking yet again that this was the year she was going to quit.

But not tonight.

She leaned back in her chair, drawing on the cigarette, enjoying Jack as he began to sing his version of "Call Me Irresponsible." Speaking of irresponsible, she thought as Jack's rendition was interrupted by the ragged snores coming from Dad Shirley across the trailer, spread eagled on his recliner-throne, his head thrown back, mouth propped open and wobbling each time he exhaled an explosion of air.

She sighed heavily, reluctantly removed the burning cigarette from her mouth and balanced it on the edge of an ashtray already brimming with butts. She refocused on her screen, trying to reconcile a business that these days was no business at all.

Dad lurched awake.

"Jesus Christ!" he exploded, jerking up in the recliner, eyes blinking, as though trying to come to terms with where he was.

"For God's sake, you old shit," Gail yelled, angry that he had scared her like that. "Calm down."

"Goddamn bad dream," Dad said, struggling out of the recliner. "Dreamed about the grandkids. Grandkids falling into a pit."

"Yeah, right," Gail sneered. "You and the goddamn phantom grandkids."

"Gotta pee," Dad announced.

He grabbed his cane from where it stood against his desk and hobbled around the recliner to the bathroom near the entrance door. There was a struggle with the latch until Dad got the door open and maneuvered inside, the door closing accompanied by a loud release of gas.

Gail was reaching for the cigarette, thinking all over again at the irony of coming toward the end of her life with a man who, no matter how hard she tried, she could not stop despising; a man who daily encouraged her scorn.

Jack was mid-way through his version of "The Impossible Dream" when the trailer door burst open and a hooded figure lunged in, pointing what looked to Gail like a Beretta pistol. A scarf covered most of her face.

Jack Jones was reaching a crescendo as Gail rose from her desk, the cigarette falling from her mouth, watching as the hooded intruder in slow motion turned the gun toward her. It flashed through Gail's mind that she had lost her cigarette the moment before she was shot to death in a goddamn trailer on the edge of a quarry with Jack Jones dramatic in the background.

"Shit," was all Gail had a chance to say before the bathroom door opened, banging against the hooded assailant just as she fired. Dad, pants down around his knees, stumbled forward, cane raised. The hooded intruder wasn't fast enough to avoid the blow that sent her sprawling.

"*Get the goddamn gun,*" yelled Gail.

The hooded intruder on the floor somehow managed to hold onto the gun as Dad's cane hammered down a second time. The intruder responded to the blows by wildly firing a second time. The report froze the Shirleys in place, as though holding still long enough to ascertain if either of them had been hit.

Saved momentarily from the cane, the intruder used the Beretta to whack Dad's leg. He howled, dropping the cane, grabbing at his knee, collapsing against the wall, clearing a path for the intruder to scramble to her feet and start for the door.

"I see you, bitch," Gail called, pointing an accusing, nicotine-stained finger. "*I see you.*"

The intruder staggered out the open door. Gail waddled to a cupboard, opened it and pulled out the AK-47 semi-automatic assault weapon she had stored inside. Cradling the weapon, she stepped over Dad, screaming in pain, and went out the door. Across the plain, caught in moonlight, the darting figure. Gail raised the AK-47, gritted her teeth, and opened fire. The sound echoed loudly across the quarry, bouncing off the cliffs.

The hooded intruder was gone. Gail stopped firing and lowered the weapon. Behind her, from inside the trailer, Jack Jones sang "I've Got a Lot of Livin' To Do."

Blood trickled down Shanifa's face and into her eyes as she reached the woods beyond the quarry, crashing through underbrush, and then climbing a hill to the roadway where Maitland waited, leaning against the hood of the Ford, puffing anxiously on one of her Dunhills.

As soon as she saw Shanifa, she threw away the cigarette and rushed to her. "Jesus, look at you," she exclaimed. "Are you all right? It sounded like a war zone down there."

"Need a towel," Shanifa said.

Maitland hurried to the SUV while Shanifa slumped against the hood, pulling the scarf away from her face, taking deep breaths. Maitland came back with a towel, pressing it against Shanifa's bleeding forehead. Shanifa shook her off. "I am okay," she said.

"You don't look okay. What happened?"

Shanifa waved her hand dismissively.

"Tell me," Maitland demanded.

"I failed," Shanifa said. "They are still alive."

"Let's get out of here."

"I am going back down there," Shanifa announced, using the towel to wipe at the blood spilling down her face.

"Are you crazy? We have to leave. Now."

"No, I'm going back. This must be finished."

She threw the towel away and started forward. "Shanifa," Maitland called.

"It must be done," Shanifa said.

She came to a sudden stop, swaying, holding the gun. She turned and looked at Maitland, her face haunted and anguished.

She took one more step before she collapsed to the ground.

33

The Swede," said Inspector Walter Duke.

"The Swede?" Jean gave him a look. "You call your CI, the Swede?"

"Like the Hemingway short story."

"*The Killers*?"

"That's the one."

"Is your guy Swedish?"

"Not as far as I know."

"What's his real name?"

"That's the point, isn't it? We've stayed away from real names. He's simply the Swede. The two of you can work out names when you meet."

Late afternoon, driving north from Milton, Duke behind the wheel in his customary gray, cop-in-charge suit, Jean beside him, musing again at the insanity of agreeing to this, trying not to be nervous but betrayed by a knotted stomach as they arrived in Acton.

Duke slowed to turn right at the Main Street's single stop light and then turning left onto Willow. A parking lot was across from the old City Hall but instead of pulling into it, Duke found a spot further along the street.

He turned off the engine and said, "The Swede will meet you at the far end of the parking lot."

"Why here?"

"The way the Swede wants it."

"The Swede who isn't a Swede."

"He's waiting for you," Duke said.

"You're not coming?"

"Better if it's just the two of you."

Jean got out and started back to the parking lot. A big man walking a small dog rounded the corner and came past her. She turned into the lot and walked to the end. There was no sign of anyone you might want to call the Swede.

She moved so a pickup truck could enter. A woman got out, grimacing with pain, favoring her right leg as she hobbled toward Willow.

Jean was about to return to where Duke had parked and announce this was a waste of time when a figure darted into view and came to stop.

Doyle Parker, his unshaven face shaded by a Blue Jays baseball cap, said, "Holy shit."

————

Cai Mak confronted the Shirleys inside their trailer, Dad looking the worse for wear, Gail, as usual, trying to put the best face on things. Looking at the two of them, Cai marveled again at how he had ever been talked into associating with these two idiots. Mind you, until recently, they had run a profitable business, bearing in mind he regarded the Halton region as a bit of a backwater.

"We've got a situation here," Dad Shirley said, choosing his words carefully, trying to put the lipstick on the pig.

"What kind of situation?"

"Shanifa tried to goddamn well kill us, that's the situation in a nutshell," Gail chimed in angrily.

"You sure it was her?"

"It was her all right," Dad said. "She made an attempt to hide under a hoodie and a scarf, but it was her all right."

"She's trying to kill us and ruin our business," Gail said. "No question, as far as we're concerned, she killed Karl, stole our product, and burned down the cabin."

"Now this," Dad said "Attempted murder." He rose to his feet to emphasize the point, leaning hard on his cane. "This damn woman is dangerous. She's got to be stopped."

A silence fell over the room. Outside, Cai could hear the grinding sound of rock-crushing machinery. He asked, "Do you make any money working this place?"

"It's a small operation," Dad conceded. "One of the few privately owned quarries left in operation. This one's just about played out."

"Why we rely on product," Gail said. "Now this ungrateful bitch Shanifa is threatening everything we've all worked for."

"I know you're pissed," Dad said, addressing Cai. "Can't say I blame you, but we were running a good business until this trouble started. The fact is, the longer Shanifa's out there, the more difficult it will be for us—and you—to get restarted."

Cai didn't like to admit it, but they had a point. "Let me see what I can find out," Cai said finally.

"Meantime, we'd like to get up and running again as soon as possible," Gail said.

"Would you now?"

"We need more product," Gail continued. "The whales are calling. You can supply us with product. We need you to do that."

Dad added, "Question is, will you?"

"Let's get this other thing settled," Cai said. "Then we can talk." He nodded at the two of them. "I'll be in touch."

And then he was gone. Gail looked over at Dad. "Bastard," she said.

"Son of a bitch," he said.

34

Doyle Parker looked confused. "The what?"

He was jiggling around, favoring one foot and then the other, a curious, nervous dance in front of a still-astonished Jean.

"The Swede. The CI."

"Jesus, will you keep it down?" His eyes darted around as though someone might be listening. "And I'm no goddamn Swede."

"I can't do this," she announced.

That calmed him somewhat, made him focus. "What do you mean?"

"Not with you," she said.

"Do they know about you and me?"

"What's that mean? There is no 'you and me.'"

"That you're Daye's cousin. That I'm married to her."

Jean shook her head. "I don't think so. Not unless you told them."

"Me? How could I tell them anything? But it's just like them," Doyle said miserably. "Throwing us together, pulling a stunt like this."

"It's not going to work," Jean said.

"Listen, I don't like it any more than you."

"Tell me what this is about."

"I work for the Shirleys," Doyle stated.

"Tell me something I don't know."

"Yeah, well, that quarry is a front. They're bringing in women from Toronto and then pimping them out."

"And you're involved?"

Doyle hesitated and shrugged. "You might say that, yeah."

"If you're working with the Mounties, what's stopping them from moving in on the Shirleys?"

"I don't know. Maybe they don't think I'm a reliable witness." He gave her a thin smile. "Maybe they think you can do better."

Doyle fished a pack of cigarettes out of his jacket and lit one. He took a deep drag, blew out a cloud of smoke before he said, "Anyway, I'm not so sure this is going to work."

"Why not?"

"One of the women, an African named Shanifa, me and Karl, we took her to a whale in Toronto. The next thing, the whale is dead, and Karl, the guy who was supposed to pick her up, he's dead from a gunshot wound. After that, the product working for Dad and Gail took off."

"Product?"

"The whores. We call them product. They burned down their cabin."

"I saw that."

Doyle looked at her suspiciously. "You were out there? What were you doing?"

"There was an Asian man snooping around. Any idea who that was?"

"That would be Cai Mak," Doyle said.

"Who is he?"

"Cai's the boss man. The big kahuna. The son of a bitch you don't mess with."

"Where did the women go?"

Another shrug. "Who knows? The Shirleys think Shanifa is behind all the shit that's gone down. One thing is for sure, Cai Mak isn't happy. That's why you saw him out here. He's been sniffing around making life difficult for me and the Shirleys. They are scared shitless that he's gonna put them out of business because of the way they have screwed things up."

"How much of this have you told the Mounties?"

"Haven't told them shit," Doyle said. He threw his cigarette butt down on the ground and used his foot to stomp it. "The thing is, I'm thinking this through, what's happening could work out nicely for you—and for me."

"How's that?"

"With everything in limbo, fresh blood, a woman with street smarts, well, they might be open to something like that. Know what I mean?"

"Can you get me in?"

"Before I agree to anything, there's something I need from you."

"What's that?"

"My wife. I want to know where she is. I want to see her."

"That's not going to happen."

"She's with you, isn't she?"

"No, she isn't."

"That's the deal, okay? You help me with Daye, I help you with the Shirleys."

"I told you, that's not going to happen. I don't want you anywhere near her."

"Then screw it."

Doyle walked away.

———————

"How did it go?" Inspector Walter Duke demanded when Jean got back into the car.

"It didn't," Jean replied.

Duke looked surprised. "What do you mean, it didn't?"

"Just what I said," Jean snapped. "The guy's a prick. Let's get out of here."

"What the hell," Duke said.

"Please, go."

Duke gave her another look but then started the engine and put the car into gear. He backed into the lot. There was no sign of Doyle Parker. Duke drove forward onto Willow, turning right and then left, driving south away from town.

"Why didn't you tell me who it was?" Jean asked angrily.

"The Swede," Duke stated. "He's the Swede."

"He's not the Swede." Jean's voice was even angrier. "He doesn't even know he's supposed to be the Swede."

"That's how I know him."

"His name is Doyle Parker. He's been assaulting my cousin. He knows me. I know him. I don't want to have anything to do with him."

"We could still make this work," Duke said.

"I don't think so," Jean said. "He wants me to tell him where his wife is. He's already threatened to kill her. There's no way I'm going to let him anywhere near her."

"I'll talk with him," Duke said.

"Forget it," Jean said. "I'm not having anything to do him."

Duke dropped Jean off at the spot back in Milton where she had parked her car. "I'll be in touch," was all he said before driving off.

She should never have become involved in this craziness, Jean thought as she drove home. Stupid, careless decision on her part.

Right now, though, she was more concerned for Daye's safety than anything else. Doyle was out there, angry and looking for her. She doubted their unexpected encounter would put him off.

She parked and then unlocked the front door and entered the silent house. Except it shouldn't be silent. There should be an excited German Shepherd greeting her. But Otis did not appear. She saw the note on the counter when she entered the kitchen.

"I'm back with apologies," the note read. "I've taken Otis for a walk. He seemed to want one. Back shortly."

It was signed, Daye.

Jean had an instant to feel relief before she heard a sound behind her. She had another instant to regret not locking the front door as she came in, to regret she didn't take her gun. Not much time, though. The shattering pain obliterated all thinking, a blast furnace of hurt exploding into black.

An end to wishing.

35

Hum and rattle; rattle and hum.

The background sounds as Jean more or less regained consciousness, tossed back and forth against a hard metal surface. She opened her eyes into a pitch-black world. It took her a moment to realize that she was blindfolded and that the reason she could not move her arms was because her hands were bound behind her.

And then she understood she was lying in the back of a moving vehicle making a sharp turn that threw her even harder against the wall. She tried to brace herself as the vehicle bumped and jerked along for a few minutes before abruptly turning again and coming to a stop.

A door opening and slamming closed and then a door behind her scraping open, hands grabbing her ankles and dragging her back and out of the vehicle before tossing her to the ground. The blindfold was ripped away and Jean found herself blinking into moonlight immediately blotted by the dark shape of Doyle Parker. His stale breath choked her throat when he leaned close and said into her ear, "Tell me where she is or I'm going to kill you."

"I told you, I don't know," Jean said. "She was staying with me but then she was gone. I haven't seen her since."

"You're lying."

He jerked Jean to her feet so that she could see the moonlit cliff, the half-light reflecting off a water-filled pit. She was back at the Hidden Quarry where the bodies of the young women had been found and where her body was about to end up.

Doyle dragged her to what Jean imagined was the cliff edge. The water was a black shadow far below. Doyle pressed a gun against her head.

"Here's what's going to happen," he hissed into her ear. "You're going to tell me where I can find my wife. You're going to tell me or so help me I'm going to blow your head off and then drop you into the water and who knows if they'll ever find you."

"Is that what you did with those three women, Doyle?"

"Don't know what you're talking about," Doyle said.

"Sure you do, Doyle. Three women who crossed you. You dumped their bodies into the water, just like you're threatening to do with me."

"That wasn't me, I had nothing to do with that," Doyle said. But he was sounding uncertain when he said it. "Don't know what you're trying to pull, but it's not going to work."

"Isn't it, Doyle? The Mounties have been protecting you until now. But you kill one of their own and all bets are off. I've gone missing. Maybe they won't find my body, but then maybe they will. One way or the other, who do you think they're going to come looking for? And then they're going to link you to those three dead women. And you're going to be in jail for the rest of your life and there are no more chances with Daye."

That caused Doyle to hesitate. The gun barrel wasn't so hard against her head now.

"Tell you what you do," Jean went on. "Untie me and we start over. We work together like they want us to. At the same time, you and I talk. I listen to your side of things. Maybe I'm missing something. Let's find out. When it's over, I'll do my best to help you with Daye."

"What do you mean you'll help?"

"It means there are no guarantees with her, but by the time this is over, you're going to be a changed man."

"Am I?"

"You'd better be or else it won't matter whether I'm dead or alive, you'll never get her back."

"Shit," he said in a broken voice.

"Let's start changing things," she said.

"You're not going to say anything? Not to the Mounties? To Daye?"

"This stays between us," she said. "The two of us working things out and then moving forward. No one but us."

"I'm so goddamn screwed up." Doyle sounded exhausted, lost. The tough guy was gone.

"This is where you stop screwing up," she said. "This is where it ends."

For a time, nothing happened. She began to fear that he wasn't going free her. Then he was fumbling with the knots binding her, swearing in exasperation.

"Can you get them?" she asked.

"Just a goddamn minute," he said impatiently.

She strained around to see him withdraw a switch-blade from his pocket. It had been a long time since she had seen one of those. The long blade sprang open. He used it to cut her hands free. She turned to see him looking surprisingly helpless. Not what she would have expected.

He shrugged uncomfortably and said, "Okay, what now?"

"Now you stop acting like an asshole," she said.

"Sometimes I get pissed and lose it," he conceded.

"I think that's what is called anger management," Jean offered.

"Yeah? What's that? What'd you just call it?"

"Never mind. For now, set something up with the Shirleys. Meanwhile, I'll get in touch with Duke and tell him we're on."

Doyle nodded. "He really called me the Swede, huh?"

"He did."

"Jesus, that pisses me off. I'm no goddamn Swede."

"Don't worry about it," Jean said. "What Duke calls you is the least of your problems."

Doyle actually broke out a smile. "You got that right, lady. You think I'm bad, wait 'till you meet the Shirleys."

36

It was nearly one in the morning by the time Jean walked in the door.

Otis leapt to his feet to greet her. Daye sat in darkness at the kitchen table. "I was worried something had happened to you," she said.

"I'm all right," Jean said, going to the cupboard for a glass.

"You don't look all right," Daye offered.

Jean filled her glass with water and then took a long drink. She began to feel a little better. Her headache was subsiding.

"I tripped over a root running with Otis this morning. It looks worse than it is."

"Should you go to the hospital?"

"I'll see how I am in the morning," Jean said. "If I'm not feeling better, I'll get you to drive me over."

"You sure you don't want to go now?"

"Right now, all I want is a shower and a glass of wine."

"Take your shower," Daye said with a smile. "I'll pour the wine."

She stood under the hot shower spray, luxuriating in the warmth of the water, deciding whether to tell Daye about Doyle Parker, determining that wasn't a good idea, not right now.

Doyle was a dangerous, unpredictable psychopath, lacking the charm usually associated with the type. She did not want to think about how close he had come to throwing her off that quarry cliff. She shouldn't be mixed up with him, but getting mixed up had been part of saving her ass. It also had to do with protecting Daye. At least, that's what she told herself.

She turned off the shower and stepped out onto the bath mat, reaching for a towel.

But there was something else as well, something Walter Duke had inadvertently touched on: the adrenaline rush, the release from the somewhat boring routine of her life in Milton, the sense of a return to action, of feeling very much alive among people who might easily kill her.

She must be crazy, she thought, drying herself with the towel. Absolutely, totally bonkers.

As she dressed, shards of pain shot through her head. She slumped down, taking deep, relieving breaths. When the pain diminished somewhat, she stumbled into the bathroom for an Advil.

Back in the bedroom, she picked up the phone and poked out the number she had been given. Inspector Walter Duke answered almost immediately. "Do you ever call when I'm awake," he said sleepily.

"That's no fun," Jean said.

"I wasn't expecting to hear from you," he said.

"I'm full of surprises."

"Yes, I'm beginning to understand that."

"I've spoken again to Doyle Parker."

"And?"

"He's going forward with us."

"You're back in," Duke said.

"I'm in," Jean said.

"Good news."

"I wonder about that," Jean said.

Downstairs, Daye had the wine ready. They sat in the living room. Otis joined her on the sofa he wasn't supposed to be on. She sipped at her wine. It didn't help.

Daye said, "You haven't asked me why I left."

"No," Jean agreed.

"I'm sorry," Daye said. "I got really scared that Doyle was going to find me. I phoned Peter. He's out of the hospital. He insisted on coming around and picking me up."

"This is the guy you've been seeing."

"Peter Wilkes. That's right."

"The married guy you think Doyle beat up."

"Peter has left his wife," Daye said. "He wants us to be together."

"You said something about another woman he was also seeing."

"That's over," Daye said with certainty.

"Okay." Jean couldn't keep the skepticism out of her voice.

"He's…he's coming… here in a few minutes. To pick me up."

"At this hour?"

"He's being insistent," Daye said.

"I'm not sure how wise that is, but if it's what you want..." Jean allowed her voice to trail off.

"He's rented a place in Toronto. No one knows about it. I'll be safer with him."

"Are you sure?"

She forced a wan smile. "I'm not sure of anything these days."

Peter Wilkes arrived ten minutes later, his head bandaged, his face swollen in shades of red and black. He looked almost embarrassed to be there. "Hey," he said when Jean opened the door. "You probably know I'm Peter."

"And you probably know that I'm Jean," she said. "Come in."

"Sorry, to do this so late," he said stepping past her into the house.

"It's all right," Jean said.

Daye came out of the kitchen looking anxious. "You look awful," she said.

"It looks worse than it feels," Peter said.

"I'll get my things," she said.

Jean invited Peter to sit down, asked if he wanted anything. "No, I'm fine," he said, seated uncomfortably on a kitchen chair, a pale, athletically slim man in his early forties, a runner, Jean surmised.

"I—I want to thank you for taking care of Daye," he said.

"I didn't do much," Jean said.

"You scared the shit out of her husband—her ex-husband. That's more than I've been able to do, obviously—or the police."

"Just be careful," Jean said. "Doyle is still out there."

"Yeah, well, look at me. You don't have to tell me to be careful."

"I've talked to the police here, and they're keeping an eye on him. But still…"

"I understand," Peter said.

"Leave me your address and phone number, will you?"

"Of course."

While Peter wrote out his address, Daye came back to the kitchen with her overnight bag, trailed by Otis. She embraced Jean. "Thank you."

"Let me know when you get settled."

Peter was on his feet taking Daye's bag. They went out the door. Jean stood on the threshold, holding Otis, watching them get into Peter's BMW.

She closed the door, heard them drive away, uncertain whether she should have let them go. Uncertain about so much.

An uncertain life.

———————

Down the street, the BMW picked up speed, zipping past the pickup truck parked at the curb.

Doyle Parker caught the flash of his wife's profile in the passenger seat. He doused his cigarette, started the truck's engine and pulled out of the parking spot.

Following.

37

Early morning sunlight cast the Toronto cityscape in gold; a rich city bathed in gold. Too rich for his blood, Doyle thought as he came in on the Gardiner Expressway following Daye and her boyfriend through the thick rush-hour traffic.

The sun was fully up by the time the Lexus found a parking spot on a residential street a block south of St. Clair Avenue. He rolled past the two as they entered one of the duplexes half way along the block.

Unable to find parking on their street, he drove around the corner until he found an empty space. How could you live in a neighborhood where there was no goddamned parking, he wondered?

A fashionable-looking couple came along pulling a small white dog on a leash. The guy looked tanned and fit, slowing to give Doyle the stink eye as though to ask what a lowlife like Doyle Parker in a goddamn pickup truck was doing in his fashionable neighborhood. At least that's what Doyle imagined and that's what started him worrying about someone calling the cops, the last thing he needed, having attracted more than enough attention from cops, thanks very much.

He got out of his truck and lit a cigarette. He'd walk around a bit, part of the street scene, not so obvious as he would be sitting in a parked truck. He dragged on the cigarette as a jogger looped past. Another look.

The bastard probably didn't like him smoking. Well, that was too goddamn bad, wasn't it?

He started along the street, holding the cigarette at his side so it wasn't quite so obvious. He reached the end of the block. Daye and her lover were in that duplex with a porch that could use a paint job.

Crossing the street, intending to walk past their place, Doyle relaxed. This was fine, a guy smoking a cigarette, minding his own business out for a morning walk. Who could possibly be suspicious?

He slowed in the middle of the empty street, taking one more drag before getting rid of the cigarette, allowing the heat of anger to boil up, imagining what he would do with his wife when he got hold of her, dismissing any assurances he might have given that bitch Jean Whitlock about anger whatever-you-call-it.

His furies cut off the outside world, the world he should have been paying attention to, the world that allowed the SUV he didn't see to slam into him, simultaneously launching him and his cigarette into the air.

Doyle bounced across the SUV's hood, smashing the windshield before flying over the top and landing on the street with a bone-crunching thump.

Shanifa, behind the wheel of the vehicle, saw none of this, too busy trying to maintain control at the moment of impact. As she sped away, she glanced in the rear-view mirror to satisfy herself that Doyle's body lay crumpled at the side of the street.

In the gutter, she observed as she turned a corner. Exactly where Doyle should be.

———

One of the great things about having Otis in her life, Jean observed, was that no matter how you were feeling, you still had to get up in the morning and walk him. It focused the day, she allowed, following Otis into the Milton Fair Grounds. You had to think of someone other than yourself—someone you had to consider before considering anything else. A dog gave you a reason for being—much like children, she suspected. Only better.

Maybe.

A dog could also alert you to imminent danger in a way no child ever could. Otis's fur bristled, his jaws working themselves into a low growl as Mickey Dann said, "Good morning, Jean."

Jean said to Otis, "Easy boy." And immediately he dropped to his haunches. Mickey remained in place. "I don't think he likes me."

"He's suspicious of you," Jean said.

"Me?" Mickey, all innocence.

"What a cop might be doing out at the Milton Fair Grounds this early in the morning."

"A cop might be wanting to talk to you," Mickey said.

"In that case, I won't let Otis rip your throat out."

"Much appreciated," Mickey said.

"Actually, he's a pussycat."

Mickey noted the dog's tense stillness, the dangerous glint in his eye. "I wonder about that," he said.

"You can walk with us," Jean said. "That way he can get to know you better."

That was Otis's cue to resume his forward momentum; a dog on a mission. Mickey hurried to catch up.

"You want to talk about why you haven't called me," Jean said.

"This isn't a personal visit," Mickey said.

"No?"

"Doyle Parker."

"What about him?"

"A lot of people are asking me what you are doing sticking your nose into Doyle's life."

"A lot of people? How many people?"

"Jean, what are you doing?"

"Sticking my nose. That's an interesting way to put it."

"Come on. You know what I mean."

"I have no idea what you mean."

Mickey stopped but Otis had no intention of following suit. He yanked Jean forward. Mickey called out, "Hey, we need to talk about this."

Jean halted Otis. Mickey walked to where she stood. Otis did not look happy. Jean wondered what she could safely tell Mickey.

"Don't worry. I'm working undercover for the RCMP and Doyle is their informant?"

That didn't sound right. For starters, she wasn't certain if she *was* working undercover, let alone if she should be admitting it to a Halton police detective.

"You know his wife is my cousin," Jean said aloud. "I'm trying to help her get away from him."

"Doyle is being investigated by us and by the Metropolitan Toronto Police. Your presence complicates things."

"I'm sorry if trying to protect my cousin complicates things."

"Where were you last night?"

"What difference does that make?"

"Just tell me where you were."

"I was home with Otis."

"Not in Toronto?"

"What would I be doing in Toronto?"

"Running over Doyle Parker to make sure he doesn't bother your cousin anymore?"

Jean looked at him with something like astonishment. "You're kidding."

"There is some thought it might be you."

"Is he alive?"

"Just. In St. Mike's Hospital."

"There you go. It couldn't be me."

"Why not?" Mickey asked.

"If it was me, he'd be dead."

Mickey shook his head before he said, "Can I make a gentle suggestion without you getting pissed?"

"Probably not," Jean said. "But give it a try."

"Stay away. Let the police deal with this."

"The police who might arrest me for hit and run?"

"It's a theory, that's all. Why I'm here. To make sure it doesn't go beyond theory."

"You know it doesn't, Mickey. You didn't have to interrupt Otis's walk to confirm it."

"I hope not," Mickey said.

"You know, it occurs to me that the only time I ever see you is when you need my help or when you think I killed someone."

"Or a combination thereof," Mickey said, smiling.

"I've got a dog to walk," Jean said, starting off with Otis. "Just so you know. I don't plan on killing anyone today."

"That's reassuring news," Mickey called.

Jean gave him the finger and continued walking.

38

In the waiting room outside the Intensive Care Unit at St. Michael's Hospital, one of the trauma nurses enumerated Doyle Parker's injuries: "Two broken legs, a broken left hand, fractured pelvis, dislocated shoulder, contusions to his face and torso."

The trauma nurse paused for breath. "We're still waiting for the CT scan results. That'll give us some idea of what he's done to his head."

As the toll taken by Doyle's encounter with a hit-and-run vehicle was listed, Jean tried to adopt an expression that was a combination of horror-struck disbelief and deep concern. Horror at the extent of Doyle's injuries was not hard; the deep concern was more difficult to pull off.

She had told the nursing station that she was Doyle's fiancée and practically choked on the words as they came out of her mouth.

"Is he going to be all right?"

"We're doing the best we can," the nurse answered "The doctor will be around in an hour or so. You can get an update from him."

Well, Jean wasn't about to wait around for a doctor. She was beginning to question why she had come here in the first place. Except, she kind of knew why, and the reason why as luck—or was it misfortune?—would have it, lingered by the elevators.

A large woman with a broad smoker's face, and eyes black with suspicion, the woman Jean immediately recognized—the fat woman she had seen at the burned-out cabin near the Hidden Quarry. The fat woman with the Asian man, Cai Mak. The boss man. The big kahuna.

"Jean Whitlock." A statement made in the gravelly voice you got from half a century of smoking.

"That's right," Jean said. "Who are you?"

"Gail Shirley's my name, dear."

"Doyle may have spoken to you about me."

"Doyle told us all about you. I thought I might find you here. Have you seen him?"

Jean shook her head. "The police are with him," Jean said.

"Then it's best we don't hang around," Gail said. She pressed the down button for the elevator. When they got outside, Gail stopped to light a cigarette. "I'm old enough to remember when you could smoke in a hospital," she said.

Jean watched her drag on the cigarette and then exhale. "That's better," she said.

"They're not good for you," Jean said.

Gail just looked at her. "Any idea what happened to Doyle?" she asked.

"He got hit by a car, that's all I know," Jean said.

Gail nodded. "And how did you know which hospital he was in?"

"The police called," Jean said, thinking quickly. "They must have found my number in his phone."

"Doyle told me we could use someone like you."

"You listen to Doyle?" Jean asked.

"Doyle's an asshole." Gail looked Jean up and down. "But maybe in your case he was on to something."

"Yeah?"

"Tell me," Gail said after taking another long draw on her cigarette, "what are you doing here?"

"I wanted to make sure Doyle was all right," Jean said. "And I was hoping he could tell me how to get in touch with you."

Gail allowed the beginnings of a smile. She threw away what was left of her cigarette.

Jean wasn't quite sure where they had materialized from but now there were a couple of massively built characters with the shaved heads de rigueur for young men tasked with breaking bones.

"You might have said something about not having a choice," Jean said.

"There's a choice," Gail said. "You can come or we can make you come."

"Friends of Doyle's?" Jean asked, nodding to the thugs.

"We're all friends here," Gail said.

"In that case, sure. Why not?"

A black SUV appeared with yet another guy with a shaved head behind the wheel. It stopped near Gail. Jean gave her a questioning look. "What's this?"

"We're taking you for a ride," Gail said. She said it with a smile.

"Except I need my car," Jean said.

"Good. Then you can take me for a ride," Gail said. She turned to the two massive characters lingering nearby. "Go with Ivan," she ordered. "We'll follow you."

39

With Gail seated next to her, Jean followed Ivan and his two pals in the black SUV along Lakeshore Drive, past the ranks of high-rises that had mushroomed in recent years until they reached a strip of motels Jean would have thought long gone by now. But they somehow had survived condo-obsessed developers.

Gail Shirley instructed Jean to turn left into a two-tiered motel with a neon sign that declared this was the Hav-A-Nap. There was, according to a smaller sign, a Vacancy.

Jean parked in front. As she got out, Jean saw that Ivan was already parked. He remained behind the wheel while his two companions, arms folded, leaned against the vehicle.

Gail waddled to a peeling brown door with the number nine painted on it. She produced the room key, shoved it in the lock, and opened the door.

Inside, a dismal interior, two double beds, a bureau scarred with cigarette burns, and an ancient wall-mounted television screen. Four young women dressed in gray hoodies, three in tights and one wearing jeans, sat tensely on the two beds. They looked up, startled. Startled and then frightened.

"Listen up, girls," Gail ordered in a sharp, authoritarian voice; the drill sergeant going to work on the new recruits. "This is Jean." She jerked a thumb in

Jean's direction. "She's going to be looking after you. You don't screw around with her, understand? She's running this crew. Do as she says."

Gail turned to Jean. "We'll be in touch," she said.

She opened the door and before Jean could say anything, went out. Jean stood gaping at the four women who, in turn, gaped back at her.

Jean hurried outside to where Gail had stopped to light a cigarette. "Hey, what do you think you're doing?"

Gail allowed a stream of smoke to escape into the air. "Doyle told me you can handle things."

"Yeah? What does that mean?"

"That's it. Handle things. This motel is temporary until we can move the product to a more permanent location. You'll get a schedule in the morning. The whales are calling."

"Whales?"

"The clients, honey. Make the deliveries. Do what Doyle says you can do."

Gail doused her cigarette as Ivan appeared in the SUV. It stopped in front of Gail. She swayed over, opened the passenger door and heaved herself in.

The SUV sped off, leaving a bewildered Jean.

———

The four young women resumed their startled and then fearful expressions as Jean re-entered. They looked very young. Jean said a silent prayer that they were at least eighteen before she said, "Do any of you speak English?"

Blank looks.

"*Parlez-vous francais?*"

A tiny, birdlike woman tentatively raised her hand.

"Where are you from?" Jean asked in French.

"Moroc," answered the woman."

"*Votre nom?*"

"Deeksha."

"Deeksha, *s'il vous plaît.* Help me with the names of the other women."

The birdlike young woman nodded and then pointed to the tall slim woman seated beside her. "This is Zindzi," she explained in French. "She is from South Africa."

"Zindzi," Jean repeated. The tall young woman looked even more scared.

Jean smiled and spoke to her in soft voice. "It's all right, you are safe with me."

Zindzi gave a dubious look. "Are you certain?" she said slowly in English.

"You do speak English."

"A little," she admitted.

The largest and most aggressive-looking of the four returned a fierce look as soon as Jean turned her gaze on her. Deeksha spoke to her in what sounded like Arabic. The aggressive woman responded in angry-sounding Arabic. Deeksha said to Jean, "She says her name is Maitha. She says she is from Dubai. She says she does not want to be here."

"I can't say as I blame her," Jean said.

"You have a cigarette?" Thickly accented English was spoken by the fourth woman. She was small and statuesque, with pale, flawless skin and hair the color of straw falling to her shoulders. "You have cigarettes?"

"Sorry, I don't smoke," Jean said. "What is your name?"

"I am Polina and I am from Minsk in Belarus."

"Where you learned to speak English."

"A little bit," she confirmed. "But not in Minsk."

"Where then?"

"On my back in Moscow with American businessmen."

The others chuckled.

"So Polina, Zindzi, Deeksha, Maitha, my name is Jean. I want you to gather your things."

"Why should we do that?" Zindzi demanded.

"I'm taking you away from here."

"You cannot, please, whore us out tonight," Polina said. "We have come from Montreal. We have not eaten or slept for over twenty-four hours."

"Don't worry," Jean said. "I am not going to 'whore you out,' as you say. I'm taking you to a safe place."

"Safe?" Deeksha looked confused. "What does that mean?"

"It means what it says," Jean said. "I'm taking you out of danger."

"There must be some catch," Polina said with a sneer. "Tell us what it is."

"There is no catch," Jean said.

"Why would you do that?" Zindzi demanded.

"Let's say I want to help you."

"But you are one of *them*," Polina stated defiantly.

"For now, you're going to have to trust me," Jean said. "Gather your belongings and let's get out of here."

The four women didn't look as though they for a moment believed Jean. Still, there weren't a lot of alternatives and so they gathered bags scattered around the room while Jean considered whether she was out of her mind for doing what she was about to do.

40

If the four women had doubts about their safety, those doubts evaporated as soon as they met Otis. How could anyone who lived with a dog as friendly and loving as Otis, who basked so lavishly in the attention these new arrivals provided, how could someone like that be a threat?

After Otis had been properly fussed over, Jean established Deeksha and Zindzi in the guest bedroom; Polina was housed in the den. Jean made up a bed on the living room sofa for Maitha. Once everyone was more of less settled, numerous trips made to the house's two bathrooms for much-needed cleanups, everyone gathered in the kitchen armed with water and soft drinks. Otis happily allowed more showers of attention. Jean ordered two party-size pizzas that were devoured as soon as they arrived.

In a blink, they had gone from the misery of rough, threatening overseers holding them hostage in a smelly motel room to the welcoming warmth of a pleasant home, a friendly dog, and a strange woman who offered them a clean bed and pizza.

What the hell had happened?

Jean wasn't sure either. She was supposed to infiltrate an organized sex ring. Instead, she no sooner met the young women, than she was spiriting them away and putting them up in her house. Not exactly what an undercover operative was supposed to do.

They were all safe tonight. But what about tomorrow? She would have to deal with Gail Shirley, undoubtedly furious realizing she had been betrayed. And then there was Inspector Duke, equally furious that his confidential informant had so quickly and carelessly blown her cover.

By the time they finished the pizza, it was nearing midnight. All the energy had leaked away; the women were exhausted.

"Perhaps tomorrow, the cigarettes," Polina said in a tired voice

"Tomorrow, the cigarettes," Jean agreed.

Jean got the four tucked in—a phrase she never thought she would use with a group of women—having outfitted them in various forms of night clothes. She turned off or dimmed lights and the house fell to silence. Jean retreated to the kitchen and Otis hovering by the back door.

The moon illuminated their midnight walk, tossing Otis's long shadow across passing lawns. Beneath the moon, caught in pools of light from streetlamps, overwhelmed by the silence of the night, Jean could make herself believe in the innocence of a small town—that is if you could forget the four victims of international sex trafficking back at her house hopefully falling asleep. The world came to small Canadian towns like Milton, crowding in and not always in good ways.

Sometimes at this time of night, you needed faith—and a dog.

The dog definitely, Jean decided.
Positively the dog.

41

Shanifa, dressed in black, crouching among the giant wheel loaders and the massive rock trucks behind the trailer, adjusted her ski mask, wishing the moon wasn't so full, that the wind would die down, that she hadn't screwed up the first time, forcing her to try this again.

But she was a warrior on a mission and the moon and the wind and fears of failure would not stop her. She started through the machines and as she approached the trailer, she could hear rising voices.

Gail and Dad Shirley, passionately engaged in what they did best: fighting.

Shanifa hugged against the wall hearing Gail scream at her husband: "Don't talk to me about screwing up, you bastard!"

"You've lost them!" he yelled back. "Turning fresh product over to some goddamn woman at the Hav-a-Nap, a woman you've never laid eyes on. If that isn't screwing up, I don't know what the hell is!"

They had lost product? Shanifa thought. What did that mean? She and Maitland had nothing to do with that. Were others stealing product from the Shirleys? She knew where the motel was located. She had spent time there herself.

Drawing the Beretta, Shanifa slipped around to the front of the trailer, went up the steps, took one of the deep breaths that were helpful whenever she found herself in a dangerous situation, and amid the angry shouts from inside, opened the door and pushed inside.

Under bright ceiling lights, Gail Shirley leaned over Dad straining forward in his recliner. So intent were they hurling invective at one another that initially they didn't notice Shanifa.

When Gail spotted Shanifa, she jerked back in alarm. "Jesus Christ."

As Dad Shirley craned around to see who had interrupted them, Shanifa shot him in the chest. The bullet wiped the fury off Dad's face as it knocked him back into the recliner.

Gail Shirley began to scream hysterically. Shanifa whipped the pistol across her head knocking her, sobbing and gurgling, to the floor. Shanifa then removed the plastic zip ties from her jacket, straddled the moaning Gail, roughly forced her onto her stomach, and dropped the pistol onto the nearby desk so that she could yank Gail's arms behind her and tie her wrists together.

When that was done, she pushed the gun barrel against Gail's head. "You have one chance to live," Shanifa said. "Do you understand?"

When Gail didn't immediately answer, Shanifa whacked her with the gun.

"Yes," Gail howled. "*Yes.*"

"Tell me this: who took your product?"

Gail's head was bleeding. Her voice was slurred and muffled as she said, "I don't understand."

"I heard you say women were taken from you. Who took them?"

"Jean," Gail answered.

"Jean who?"

"Whitlock. Jean Whitlock. Recommended by Doyle. I left her at the motel with four. Now they're gone."

Shanifa straightened, backed away. Gail mumbled, "What are you going to do?"

Shanifa backed to the door, opened it, and went out. The wind wailed across the flat plain of the quarry. The moon remained in place. Everything else was changing, Shanifa mused as she jumped down the steps and went around to where the rock trucks and the wheel loaders were parked.

She climbed the short ladder into the cab of the wheel loader closest to the trailer. The key was in the ignition. The engine growled to life. She fumbled with the control handles mounted to the right of her seat, made sure the shovel was in a lowered position, trying to remember what one of the young truck operators had told her about operating this machine one night as she was forced to entertain him.

The loader jerked and then lurched slowly toward the trailer. The shovel slipped beneath the trailer's underside, crunching against the siding, moving the trailer slowly forward, the steel frame buckling, wooden floor joists snapping and cracking.

Shanifa kept pressure on the gas pedal as breaking power lines attached to the roof hissed and sparked. In the moonlit darkness, the trailer shook violently, folding in on itself as the loader pushed it to the cliff edge.

At the absolute last moment, Shanifa opened the cab door and leapt from the loader. She landed hard on the ground, rising to a sitting position in time to see the trailer disappear over the edge, followed shortly by the wheel loader.

Shanifa got to her feet as a tremendous roar accompanied by a burst of white light lit the night sky. The force of the explosion sent her sprawling backwards.

She lay there, smoke and fire rising into the night as if the pits of hell had opened up. She began to laugh. She couldn't stop laughing. From somewhere behind her, figures approached. She fumbled for the gun in her belt as the figures drew closer. She raised her gun, firing into the air. The figures promptly disappeared into the darkness.

In the fiery light of the hell pit, Shanifa kept laughing.

She had never laughed so hard in her life.

42

When he got the phone call from Dash Jessup, Mickey was entangled with Dara Tate in the front seat of his car.

She had murmured that he shouldn't answer the phone. But when he saw who it was, he removed himself as best he could from her embrace.

"Doyle Parker has regained consciousness," Dash said. "I'm about to go over to the hospital. Do you want to come along? I'll wait for you if you want to be part of this."

"I'm on my way," Mickey said. When he said it, Dara moved away, curling in a corner of the seat.

"How far away are you?" Dash asked.

"I could be in town in an hour, depending on traffic," Mickey said.

"I'll meet you at St. Mike's," she said.

Mickey closed his phone. "I have to go," he said to Dara.

"You're a bastard," she said angrily, pulling her skirt back into place.

"I'm a cop," Mickey said.

"It's the same thing," she said sullenly. "You're a worse bastard than he is."

"Look, I'm sorry, but I have to go."

"I don't know what I'm doing, I really don't." She had tears in her eyes.

"That's two of us," Mickey said.

Dara glared at him and then without another word, opened the door and got out. She slammed the door hard.

He watched her flounce away.

———————

What with the traffic, it took Mickey over an hour to reach St. Michael's Hospital in downtown Toronto. He met Dash Jessup in the reception area outside the ICU. "I'm told that we can only have about fifteen minutes with him," she said punching in the code that opened the double doors to the unit.

"Have you seen him?"

"Not since they brought him in," she said.

Doyle had been transferred to a private room. Pale and unshaven, Doyle appeared curiously innocent, his face robbed of its usual anger and deceit; the bad guy reduced.

He lay amid the pulleys and wheels of traction devices, oxygen, drips, and heart monitors that kept even guys like Doyle alive.

At first, Mickey thought Doyle was asleep, but as soon as Dash said, "Hey, Doyle," his eyes fluttered open and he managed to say, "Shit."

"That's no way to greet your pals, Doyle," Dash said, seating herself in the chair beside his bed. Mickey folded his arms as he took up a position against the wall.

"Screw you," Doyle said.

"Right now, believe it or not, we're the only friends you got." Dash leaned into him, as though to let him in on a secret. "Face it, Doyle. What happened to you was no accident. Someone ran you over on purpose. Someone who wanted you dead. And you know what? You're not out of the woods yet. You're really screwed up inside, bleeding internally. You could still end up dead."

Doyle blinked a couple of times but didn't say anything.

"And you know what?" Dash continued. "No one's going to give a shit and, even worse, whoever did this to you gets away scot free. Right now, it serves a larger purpose for you to help us, but if you're dead, well, the only reason we'd keep looking for your killer is to give that person a medal for exemplary community service."

Doyle's dry, cracked lips moved. He said, "Water."

A paper cup with a straw stood on a nearby tray table. Dash nodded at Mickey who grabbed it and handed it to her. She stood and fed the straw into Doyle's mouth. He sucked on it enthusiastically. Dash withdrew the straw and said, "What about it, Doyle? Are you going to help us?"

Doyle tried a smile that didn't work. Dash fed him some more water. Doyle's eyes brightened a bit. His lips moved. "Bitch," he said.

Dash leaned closer to him. "What?"

"She's a bitch," Doyle mumbled.

"Who? Who's a bitch?"

"Bitch. Shanifa."

"Shanifa ran you over?"

Doyle nodded enough to make Mickey believed he was answering in the affirmative.

"Why would she do that to you? Why would she try to kill you?"

"Wants to kill all of us," Doyle said.

"Why?"

Mickey didn't think Doyle was going to answer. Then his lips started moving again and he said, "She took off. Probably killed Karl. Then she came back. Stole the product. The Shirleys…"

"Dad and Gail," Dash acknowledged. "What about them?"

"…running the product. Shanifa came and got them…burned down the cabin. The Shirleys don't know whether to shit or go blind."

Mickey watched Dash closely. She looked skeptical. Mickey could hardly blame her. "You mean to tell me some kid the Shirleys probably kidnapped into the sex trade escaped, taking other women with her?"

Doyle moved his head up and down.

"Now she's out for revenge? Is that it?"

Doyle moved his head some more.

"Do you know Shanifa's last name? Where we can find her?"

"That's enough." Mickey turned to see Inspector Walter Duke poised at the threshold, accompanied by two uniformed RCMP officers.

43

You said you were going to leave them alone," Maitland said to Shanifa on the way back to the house after they had delivered two of the women to their whales.

"I don't understand," Shanifa said, riding beside Maitland.

"It's all over the news. You can't keep doing this. You're going to ruin it for all of us."

"I do not know what you talk about," Shanifa said.

"You disappear last night while I'm out. You come home late and don't say anything. This morning there are two deaths at a quarry outside Georgetown. Police are saying it looks like homicide. No names have been released but it doesn't take a lot of brain power to figure out who the victims are."

Shanifa exhaled air and said in the sort of patient voice she used when explaining to Maitland what already should be evident: "As long as those people were alive, they were a threat. I missed the first time. This time I didn't. They are no longer a threat."

"Except now we have the police to deal with," Maitland countered. "They are investigating those deaths and that could lead back to us."

"How could it? We had nothing to do with what happened." Shanifa sounded a lot more confident than

Maitland thought she should. "Besides, these were bad people. The police do not care about bad people."

Maitland didn't share that point of view, but what could she say? What was done was done. There was not much she could do except live with it, and hope this was the end. Except, as they turned into the drive, it became apparent it wasn't.

"There is something else," Shanifa said as Maitland came to a stop.

"What?"

"It is not finished."

Maitland gave her a look. "What does that mean?"

"The Shirleys worked for a truly evil man who lives in the city. He will come."

"Who? Who is this 'truly evil' man?'"

"You know his name, Cai Mak. The Shirleys feared him more than anything."

"I can talk to Cai," Maitland said. "Something can be worked out."

"I don't think Cai is in the business of working things out."

"Let me at least try," Maitland asked.

"If that's what you want, but we know he is coming," Shanifa said. "We must prepare, and if necessary, stop him."

————

Good god, Mickey thought, not Fran's Restaurant.

As a teenager, he and his friends used to eat at Fran's when they visited Toronto. He wasn't aware it was still around. But there they were, two cops and an RCMP inspector seated at one of the red-plush booths in the pale-green interior, ordering coffee from a waitress—and how could you call the servers here anything else, the place was such a throwback—who appeared as old as the restaurant itself.

Walter Duke tore his hungry eyes away from the glassed displays of pie long enough to address her. "And give me a slice of your apple pie with a little vanilla ice cream, if you will, my dear," requested Inspector Duke in a jolly voice Mickey would never have otherwise associated with him.

"You've got it, luv." The waitress beamed.

As soon as she trundled off, Duke was all business. "How many times do I have to request that you people stay away from Doyle Parker," he said, fixing a glare on the two detectives.

Dash Jessup was unfazed. "Your guy is the victim in a hit-and-run case. I was following that up when you appeared with your two thugs—"

"Those are highly respected uniformed officers you're talking about," Duke interrupted angrily.

"—thugs, before you had us practically ejected from the hospital."

Duke started to say something but then the waitress was back with his apple pie and ice cream. Immediately, Duke returned to the character he played in places like Fran's, the jolly aging lawman, delighted at the support—not to mention the apple pie—from the public.

"Looks wonderful, dear," he said, his eyes dancing over the pie. "Thank you so much."

"Let me know if you need anything else, luv." The waitress beamed even brighter.

Duke gave the pie a longing look, before lifting his head and returning to the business at hand. "All right, there's no sense in sitting here finger pointing," he said.

"When you could be eating your apple pie," Dash interjected.

Duke ignored her and continued, "What I'd like from the two of you is a summation of the information you may have received from Parker."

"A summation," Dash repeated, as though she couldn't quite believe he had used the word.

"Particularly anything he might have said about the informant he's been working with."

"Let me get this straight," Dash said. "Your informant is working with—an informant?"

"Parker wasn't giving us what we needed," Duke explained. "We have brought in someone we thought could assist him."

"But?" Dash raised and lowered her eyebrows questioningly.

"But now that informant seems to have gone off our radar."

"You've got one informant in the hospital, not talking, and a second informant missing. Have I got all that right?"

Duke cast another longing glance in the direction of the pie. "Which is why anything Parker gave you could be helpful."

Dash sat back and with a straight face said, "Doyle didn't give us shit, and I don't imagine he gave you anything, either."

"He's unconscious again." Duke had raised his fork preparing to attack the pie. "They're not sure about his prognosis."

"That's too bad," Dash said. She was good cop, Mickey reflected, meeting the high bar for excellence: knowing how to convincingly lie through your teeth.

"I don't like cold apple pie." Duke threw down his fork and sighed heavily. "I should have told her to heat it up."

Outside Fran's, they watched Inspector Duke march smartly to the unmarked black sedan that had pulled up on the street. Duke with a quick wave slipped into the back and the sedan sped away into the afternoon traffic.

"You see that, Mickey?" Dash nodded at the departing car. "You joined the wrong force. You join the Mounties and you get a driver."

"But then you wouldn't be nice to me, Dash. And you would tell me fibs about what you got out of Doyle Parker."

"I'm not so sure about this Shanifa thing myself," Dash said. "Are you?"

"It explains what happened to Doyle. Not to mention the Shirleys."

"It burns my ass," Dash said. "These Mountie assholes keep living on a reputation they haven't deserved for years. They don't get their man or their woman.

They're a bunch of incompetent assholes." She grinned at Mickey. "If you ask me."

"What do you want to do?"

"For starters, give our apple-pie-eating-nitwit Mountie inspector as little as possible."

"Okay. But what?"

"We run down the one lead Doyle gave us."

"Shanifa," Mickey said.

"Shanifa," Jessup agreed.

44

Of the four women, it was soon apparent that the Ukrainian, Polina, was the most difficult. The others were pussy cats, Jean surmised. Polina was making up for the others' good natures.

It began with the cigarettes. Polina kept bothering her for smokes to the point where Jean finally went out and bought her a pack. "But you don't smoke them in the house," Jean admonished.

An hour later, Jean caught Polina smoking in the house. "The window was open," Polina protested.

Next, it was the gold ring Polina's late fiancé had given her before he died at the hands of the secret police. She must have left it at the motel. If Jean could drive back there to retrieve it, she would be most appreciative. She did not know how she would live without that ring, she wept. Jean noticed the others rolling their eyes in the face of Polina's melodramatics.

"Tell you what," Jean said. "I'll drive out to the motel and look for your ring, if you promise me you aren't going to smoke in the house."

"I do *not* smoke in the house." Polina appeared outraged.

Jean folded her arms. Polina flounced around. "All right, all right," she announced. "I do not smoke in the house."

"You have to promise," Jean said.

"Promise, *promise*." Polina made a disgusted face. "On the grave of my mother, I promise."

"You told me your mother is still alive, living in Minsk," Zindzi said.

"Go to hell," Polina said.

Actually, Jean was happy for the excuse to get away for a couple of hours. Four fearful young women, unsure where they were or who was taking care of them, anxious about their futures, worried that someone was coming after them, yet enthusiastic for talk and food—definitely food—and to feel free after being locked up, well, all that could get on the nerves of someone used to being alone.

Her cellphone sounded on the seat beside her. She pressed the voice activation on her steering wheel and a voice emitted from her radio speaker saying, "Is this Jean?"

"Yes. Who's this?"

"The guy you're working for as of this morning."

"That's interesting," Jean said. "I didn't know I was working for anyone."

"You were employed by Gail and Dad Shirley. But no longer."

"Supposing that's true, why aren't I working for them?"

"They are dead," the voice said flatly.

Jean paused, not sure what to make of what she was hearing. "Are you sure about this?" she asked finally.

"Apparently you haven't listened to radio or television this morning."

"I haven not heard anything," Jean said. "What happened?"

"They were murdered last night."

Jean was trying to absorb this news as she drove. "Are you there?" the voice asked.

"Yes," Jean said. "Let's assume what you're telling me is true. What do you want?"

"I'm at the motel. You were supposed to be here with product."

"I've moved them," Jean said.

"And why would you do that?"

"I didn't think they were safe there."

"Where are they now?"

"In a safe place."

"Given what's happened, you must have had some sense that the Shirleys were in danger," the voice said. "Am I correct when I say that?"

"Put it this way, I've been around long enough to realize the women weren't safe. But I had no idea that anything was going to happen to them. They had just hired me."

"Thanks to a recommendation from Doyle Parker."

"That's right," Jean said.

"Who is now in hospital after a hit and run accident."

"You think what happened to Doyle and the death of the Shirleys—what? They're linked?"

"Something is happening," the voice said. "We must talk as soon as possible."

"I'm just coming up to the motel now," Jean said.

"I will meet you there," the voice said.

45

When Jean turned into the Hav-A-Nap there was no sign of anyone.

Jean parked and entered the motel office. The elderly reception clerk looked as though he had gone a long time between meals, and too long since he had shaved, and neglected washing his lank gray hair far too long. He gave Jean a disinterested glance. "What can I do for you?"

"Tell me your name," Jean said.

"Milton. Don't call me Milt," Milton admonished.

"Named after the town?"

"There's a town called Milton?"

"Milton, there were four young women staying with you the other night."

"Whores," Milton interrupted.

Jean ignored the description. "One of the ladies left an item behind when she checked out."

"What would that 'item' be?" asked Milton.

"What did you find after they exited the room?"

"Didn't find nothing," Milton said.

"You didn't find a ring?"

"Nothing includes a ring," Milton said.

"Do you mind if I take a look?"

"You're not going to find anything."

"No? You're sure about that?"

"Take a look for yourself, makes you feel any better." He reached around and withdrew a room key from one of the mail boxes lining the wall. "Number nine—and don't use the bathroom. Place has just been cleaned."

Jean went out along the walkway until she found room nine. She used the key to open the door and step in. The gloomy interior was a lot neater than it was the last time she saw it, suggesting no one would have left a ring or if they did, it was long gone.

She searched the drawers but found nothing. A sound came from behind her. She turned to find a tall Asian man standing in the doorway. His head was shaved. He wore glasses and a long black coat. He gave her a smile and said, "Hello, Jean."

The same man she had seen at the quarry with Gail Shirley.

Jean closed the drawer she had just opened and straightened. The Asian man stepped into the room, closing the door. Jean didn't like that. "A chance to talk in private," the Asian man said.

"We can start with your name," Jean said.

The Asian man produced a crooked smile. "You're not wearing a wire are you, Jean?"

"Why would I be wearing a wire?"

"Maybe because you're working with the cops."

"Yeah, well, I'm not working with the cops and I'm not wearing a wire, and I still don't know anything about you, so how do I know you're not wearing a wire and you're not working with the cops?"

The crooked smile widened. "Cai Mak, and I am not wearing a wire."

"Do they call you Charlie?"

"No one calls me Charlie." The smile was gone.

"So where do we go from here, Charlie?"

"I see." The smile was back but thinner this time. "You are trying to antagonize me."

"Not at all," Jean replied. "A slip of the tongue, that's all."

"Going forward, I prefer to be called Cai."

"Are we going forward?"

"There have been disruptions, Jean. You can help me get things back on track."

"Is that a fact?"

"That is if you wish to continue."

"Why wouldn't I?"

His smile was a little less thin. "I took a chance and against my better judgement, delivered new product to the Shirleys."

"You mean women, don't you?"

"Now that product is missing. I want it back. I need you to give me the whereabouts of these… women."

"Like I said before, I'm concerned about their safety, particularly in light of what happened to Doyle and now, you tell me, the Shirleys."

"They will be safe with me, I assure you."

"I can't imagine anyone who calls women 'product,' can or should be entrusted with their safety."

Cai Mak abruptly didn't look so pleasant. There were no more smiles, thin or otherwise. "Don't play with me, Jean. Tell me where the women are."

"You're not being nice, Charlie," Jean said.

"And I am particularly not nice when you call me Charlie."

His hand suddenly gripped her neck, pushing her against the wall so that she could hardly breathe.

"When I ask you something, you tell me," Cai Mak said in a preternaturally calm voice. "The whereabouts of the women."

"Stop it," a voice said. The door was open framing a small woman in black, her head covered by a hoodie, pointing a Beretta.

Cai turned, letting go of Jean. "Shanifa," she called out. "My name is Jean Whitlock. I can help you."

Shanifa allowed a quick look of surprise. How would this woman named Jean Whitlock know her? But there was no time to think about that. Cai Mak was lunging for her.

She shot him.

It was if Cai had been punched in the chest. He dropped to the floor. Shanifa turned the gun on Jean. She had just enough time to say, "Shanifa, don't."

Shanifa pulled the trigger.

There was a hollow click. No shell in the chamber. The clip was empty.

Shanifa reacted fast, swinging the Beretta, striking Jean a glancing blow. As Jean staggered, trying to stay on her feet, Shanifa wheeled out the door.

By the time Jean recovered and got outside, Shanifa was sprinting across the parking lot. Jean, her head spinning, started after her. Beyond the parking area, a narrow pathway ran along the top of a slope falling to a strip of vacant land ending at the choppy gray waters of Lake Ontario. Jean caught a glimpse of Shanifa, a moving black shadow, far down the path. A moment later, she disappeared.

Jean's vision remained blurry as she re-crossed the parking lot, quiet despite the ruckus in the motel room. The door to number nine was open. How the hell was she going to explain all this? How she ended up in a suburban motel room with a possible dead man?

She needn't have worried—or worried too much—because the Asian man in the long coat who demanded to be called Cai...

That man was gone.

"What the hell?" Jean turned to see Milton, the desk clerk in the doorway.

"Milton," she said.

"What's going on here?"

"I couldn't find the ring," Jean said, brushing past him.

"You messed up the bed," he called after her. "I hope you stayed out of the bathroom."

46

By the time Shanifa reached the strip mall further along Lakeshore Avenue where she had parked, she had calmed, relieved that the Jean Whitlock woman had given up the chase, wondering if she had killed Cai Mak, angry with herself for not checking the Beretta's magazine before starting out. But then she had not anticipated the mess she found herself confronted with, having intended only to check out the motel where she suspected any new arrivals might be held.

Shanifa got into the SUV, started the motor, swallowed the contents of the water bottle she had brought with her, took some more deep breaths before driving back onto Lakeshore. It would be fine, she decided as she drove. With any luck Cai Mak was dead and they would have nothing more to fear.

Except maybe that woman at the motel. Jean Whitlock?

Yes. That was it.

What was Jean Whitlock doing with the evil Cai Mak? And what kind of ongoing threat did she present?

Jean Whitlock had been lucky once. She would not be so lucky the next time.

———

Maitland was out with deliveries, quieting the call of the whales, so that when Shanifa got home, she had the preternaturally silent house to herself. In the kitchen, she found only a bit of sparkling water left in the fridge. She poured the water into a glass and then went into the living room, draining the glass before slumping down on the sofa, exhausted and frustrated.

Not to mention pissed off that someone had finished the sparkling water.

One of the good things about Canada, the sparkling water. Also, the many whales willing to pay lots of money for sex. Of course, that was true the world over, even in places where sparkling water was hard to come by.

The Beretta pressed uncomfortably against her stomach. She pulled it out and laid it on the coffee table, reminding herself to be sure to replace the clip. She went upstairs to where she had hidden her list. She sat on the bed, pen poised over Cai Mak's name. She put a question mark beside it. Below Cai Mak she added another name in careful block letters:

Jean Whitlock.

She finished writing when she heard the sound of a car outside.

Shanifa rose from the sofa and went to the window. Down on the street, an innocuous-looking sedan had pulled up at the curb.

Maitland had told her that if a car in this neighborhood looked so anonymous that you might not pay attention to it, it could only mean one thing.

Cops.

47

Glen Petrusiak was on the phone to Mickey. "This may be nothing, but I was just talking to my cousin at the Organized Crime Enforcement Unit at Toronto Police. They've been looking into suspicious activity out of a house in Toronto. The owner is a woman named Maitland Tompkins."

"Okay," Mickey Dann said.

"He says there are four or five women working out of there. They haven't got names for everyone, but he says one of them they've particularly had their eye on—a beautiful young black woman who goes by the name Shanifa."

"The woman Doyle Parker says ran away from the Shirleys."

"Could be the same one," Petrusiak said. "What do you think we should do?"

"Let's drive into Toronto. I'll pick you up in twenty minutes."

"You don't think we should alert the Toronto cops?"

"Let's take a look for ourselves first," Mickey said.

"Yeah, I guess so," Petrusiak said glumly.

"You okay?"

"I'm fine," Petrusiak said. "Get here as soon as you can."

———————

On the 401 highway they got caught in the bumper-to-bumper traffic that drove Mickey crazy. Petrusiak, beside him, slumped against the passenger door not saying much of anything.

"Goddamn traffic," Mickey said by way of making conversation.

"You say that every time we drive into Toronto," Petrusiak said.

"That's because there's never a time when it isn't goddamn traffic," Mickey said. "Worse than Los Angeles, they say."

"They say," Petrusiak replied, sounding glummer than ever.

Mickey eyed the eighteen-wheeler transport maneuvering into his lane. "You sure you're all right?"

"Why should you give a shit?"

"For God's sake, Glen, we're partners. We have our differences—"

"Yeah, we sure as hell do," Glen snapped.

"What's that supposed to mean?"

"What do you know about what's going on with Dara?" Out of nowhere, suddenly shrinking the interior of the car.

"Whoa," Mickey said. "Where did that come from?"

"She says she was talking to you about me."

Mickey thought, What the hell was Dara saying? Out loud, he said, "She said that?"

"That's what she said. The two of you were talking."

"News to me," Mickey said.

"You weren't talking to her about me?"

"We talked that day at the quarry when we were with Jean."

"That's it? That's the only time the two of you talked?"

"What's going on between you and Dara, anyway?" Mickey, trying to divert the conversation.

"I don't know," Petrusiak said, sounding unexpectedly helpless. "I don't know what the hell's going on. Goddamn women, honestly."

"Yeah, I hear you," Mickey said.

Petrusiak was reduced to silence. Mickey finally turned off the 401, driving south on Allen Road. When he turned onto Eglinton, Petrusiak said, "She's seeing someone."

Mickey felt his stomach drop. "I'm sorry?" He concentrated on the road.

"She's seeing someone."

"How do you know that?"

"I'm wondering if she's seeing you."

"Is that what you wonder, Glen?"

"Yeah, I do wonder, Mickey. She says she talked to you. You say she didn't talk to you."

"Not exactly evidence that would hold up in court."

"Well, we're not in court, are we? We're in a car, driving to make an arrest."

"Is that what we're doing? Making an arrest?"

"You're driving the car and you're not exactly denying anything."

"What do you want me to deny?"

"That you're fucking my fiancée."

Mickey was having trouble swallowing. He said, "I'm not fucking anyone."

More silence.

As they turned onto the street where Maitland Tompkins lived, Mickey said, "Reach into the glove box, will you, Glen? I think I left my ID in there."

"You don't carry it with you?" Petrusiak, accusatory.

"Just take a look, will you?"

Petrusiak reached forward and opened the glove compartment. The lid dropped down and Petrusiak reached inside and pulled out a woman's black lace thong. Petrusiak held the thong in his clenched fist.

Dimly, Mickey heard Petrusiak say, "What's this?"

Quickly—too quickly—Mickey said, "They have been in there for a while. I'd forgotten about them."

"I thought you weren't fucking anyone."

"I said they've been in there for a while."

Petrusiak stared at the panties scrunched in his hand. "These are Dara's," he exclaimed.

"You're crazy." Mickey swung into a parking space beside the house, turning off the ignition and immediately exiting in hopes of putting an end to this at least until he could get his head around a reasonable explanation for an unreasonable situation. Glen, red-faced, followed Mickey out of the car, still holding the thong.

Mickey came up onto the front porch and knocked on the door, Petrusiak, steaming, right behind him. He thought he heard someone inside. He knocked again. He could hear Petrusiak, breathing hard.

"You bastard." Petrusiak spat the words out.

"Jesus, Glen, calm down, will you? We can discuss this later."

Mickey had time to glimpse a startled black woman opening the door, her mouth open in surprise, before Petrusiak grabbed Mickey by the shoulder and spun him around. There was a gun in Petrusiak's hand.

Mickey clawed for the weapon, finally shaking it out of his partner's hand. Petrusiak screamed invective as he tried to knee Mickey in the groin. Mickey hit him in the face. Petrusiak fell back but managed to grab the lapels of Mickey's suit jacket so that they both tumbled together down the porch steps onto the walkway.

Petrusiak landed with a howl of pain. Mickey came down on top of him. The fall had winded Petrusiak enough so that Mickey was able to twist the detective's arm behind his back. Vaguely, he was aware of neighbors across the street.

Petrusiak continued screaming as Mickey managed to shake his handcuffs loose from his belt and then attach them to Petrusiak's wrists. He rose to his feet, breath ragged, as Petrusiak began weeping, repeating, "I'm going to kill you, you bastard. I'm going to kill you!"

Mickey suddenly remembered the woman in the house. The front door was ajar. He ran back up the steps, drawing his gun before entering. "Police," he yelled. "I'm coming in."

But there was no one in the front hall to respond. He went along the hall into a kitchen where the back door was wide open. He went out onto a wooden stoop, a patch of fenced-in yard beyond.

There was no sign of the woman.

48

Shanifa raced across the yard, scrambling over the back fence, her mind in flight mode. At all costs, get away, figure out the rest later.

She lost her balance going over the fence, fell forward onto the pavement below, using the palms of her hands to break her fall, hitting hard. Slightly dazed, her palms scrapped and bleeding, she stumbled to her feet, realizing vaguely she was on a strip of road running behind a row of houses. She reached the street, looking around for anyone who might be after her. No one.

Yet.

To her amazement, a streetcar was pulling to a stop across the street. She ran to it, and climbed aboard. Didn't matter where it was going. It was leaving. That's all that mattered. She had escaped with the two things she needed right now: her wallet and her cellphone. The wallet contained the TTC pass which got her a seat at the rear. She waited until her nerves settled and then fished her phone from her jeans pocket.

"Where are you?" she demanded when Maitland came on the line.

"I've got two of the girls, we're on our way home," Maitland said.

"Don't go there."

"Why not? What's wrong?"

Shanifa lowered her voice. "The police. I got away. But they are at the house."

"Shit," Maitland said.

"Right now, I am on a streetcar. I'm not sure where it takes me. But as soon as I stop, I will call you. Then you come and pick me up."

"Jesus, what happened?"

"I'm not sure," Shanifa said. She had regained the calm in her voice. The act of speaking made her feel stronger. "Right now, I need you to stop at an ATM machine and withdraw as much cash as you can. If they are at the house, it's a matter of time before they find our bank accounts."

"I'll do that," Maitland said.

"I will call you back," Shanifa said.

———

Shanifa remained on the streetcar for the better part of an hour as it filled and emptied, mostly with young people of all shades and sizes so that she didn't think she would stand out once the police concluded she had taken a streetcar to escape.

By then it wouldn't matter.

She got off at one of the anonymous strip malls that blighted the suburban Toronto landscape. A Tim Horton's was nearby. She went in, ordered coffee, and then sat in the back. When she finished her coffee, she phoned for a taxi. It arrived ten minutes later and she gave the driver the address of the XYZ Storage Facility on Laird, not far off Bayview Avenue.

When she got there, she paid the driver and then went to the unit she had rented shortly after installing herself at Maitland's house. She unlocked the door and pulled out the carryall she had stored there. She unzipped the bag to make sure the one hundred thousand dollars retrieved from Jason Tremblay's desk remained intact. Satisfied that the money was all there—and there was no reason to believe it wouldn't be—she rezipped the bag and carried it outside. She went down the drive and along the street until she found another Tim Horton's. She bought more coffee and then sat with the carryall while she called Maitland.

Her friend arrived thirty minutes later. Shanifa got in and Maitland immediately sped off. Two of the young women sat in the back, their faces reflecting fear.

"It will be all right," Shanifa said to them in a voice that sounded much more reassuring than she was feeling.

Maitland cast a skeptical glance in Shanifa's direction. "What's in the bag?"

"Money," Shanifa said.

"Tell me what happened." Shanifa quickly filled in the details of what appeared to be two detectives arriving at the door, one of them pulling a gun on the other, the two of them ending up wrestling on the lawn in front of the house.

"What happened then?" Maitland asked.

"I have no idea," responded Maitland. "I went out the back, over the fence, running until I saw the streetcar."

"You were lucky," Maitland said. "But this is bad. Somehow, they know where we are. I don't know how we recover from this. We're screwed."

"Where are the other two women?"

"With whales. I'm not due to pick them up for another hour."

"Very well," Shanifa said.

"Then what?"

"Then we go to the safe house."

Maitland glanced over in surprise. "What do you mean, 'safe house?' We don't have a safe house."

Shanifa smiled. "Yes, we do." It was a satisfied Cheshire cat smile, Maitland thought.

The unstoppable Shanifa.

49

Jean's house had been transformed into an oasis of tranquility, the kitchen filling with warm cooking scents, house guests busily preparing a dinner of tilapia, a tossed salad, and rice. Murderous sex trafficking overlords and gun-crazy women lurked outside. In here four women were settling into domesticity with surprising ease. The domesticity included a happy German shepherd named Otis only too pleased to accept all the extra attention being showered on him, not to mention the increase in walks provided by new pals eager to cater to his every whim.

Only Polina appeared dissatisfied, unhappy that in addition to not finding her ring at the motel, Jean had neglected to buy much-needed cigarettes.

"I am going *crazy*," she announced melodramatically. "I cannot *live* like this. I must smoke or *die*."

"Then die for God's sake," cried one of the women. "Dying will at least keep you quiet."

Polina pouted.

Dinner around the dining table featured lots of wine and raucous conversation, Jean staying mostly silent in the face of these talkative women. Best not to say anything about what had transpired at the Hav-a-Nap Motel, particularly since she had no idea what it meant for her status as confidential informant.

After dinner, she gave into Polina's pleas and with Otis in tow, trudged down to Main Street to the variety store at the corner of James and Main. That's when Inspector Walter Duke called on her cell. "You're not keeping in touch," he said in an accusatory voice.

"That's the trouble with working undercover," Jean said, pausing outside the variety store. "It's not always a good idea to be calling the Mounted Police. It tends to make the bad people suspicious."

"What's up?"

"A man named Cai Mak," Jean said.

"We are familiar with Cai Mak," Duke said. An element of excitement edged his voice. "Don't tell me you met him."

"You might say that. Who is he?"

"The biggest sex trafficker in Toronto. I'm surprised he's operating in the west, but I suppose he's expanding his operation."

"I'm surprised you didn't know the Shirleys were working for him."

"Why I wanted to put you in there," Duke said. "You've established contact?"

"Briefly," Jean said. "Where it goes from here, I don't know. I'm not certain if he sees me as an ally or a threat. We will see. But there is a problem."

"There always is," Duke said.

"There's a young woman named Shanifa out there. I think she escaped from the Shirleys. Now it appears she's looking for revenge. She's probably responsible for the deaths of Gail and Dad Shirley and she is the person who ran over Doyle Parker. This afternoon, she tried to kill Cai Mak. Me too."

"Are you all right?"

"Luckily her gun jammed," Jean said. "Otherwise…"

"I'm relieved you're all right," Duke said. "Any idea where this woman is now?"

"No idea," Jean said. "One thing is certain though."

"What's that?"

"I'm going to hear from her."

———

By the time Dash Jessup arrived on the scene, Petrusiak had settled into a sullen silence, while Mickey had stitched together a vague story about the gun drawn in pursuit of an escaping suspect.

Dash convinced the attending uniformed officers that the explanation provided by the two Halton detectives on special assignment in Toronto was good enough. This after all was not a Toronto case involving local cops. This was something that could be handled through Halton; Toronto had enough to worry about.

Dash managed to clear the uniforms out of the house and then sit Petrusiak and Mickey down. "What the hell were the two of you thinking?" she demanded. Petrusiak hung his head and didn't say anything.

Mickey said, "It was a misunderstanding, that's all."

Dash gave them both a look. "You can thank your lucky stars I was able to get here before too much damage was done. The two of you are also fortunate that this person of interest chose to hightail it out of here, and that at the end of the day, you appear to have broken up some sort of prostitution ring operating out of this house."

"Brilliant police work on our part," Petrusiak mumbled.

"Don't be an asshole," Dash said.

Petrusiak fell silent.

"Let's go through the house, see what we can find that will not only bolster the case against the people working out of here, but also give you two jerks more cover in case anyone starts asking questions." Dash delivered a glare in Petrusiak's direction. "What do you say, Glen? Can you go back to work with this guy, at least for the time being?"

Petrusiak hesitated then gave a nod.

"Okay." Dash rose decisively. "Let's get to work."

A couple of hours later, they had finished tossing the house and establishing that the woman they were looking for in addition to Maitland Tompkins was named Shanifa Mahaba.

It was Dash who found the list in what appeared to be Shanifa's bedroom. "It looks like our lady's murder list," Dash said.

Karl was the first name printed out in neat capital letters. Doyle Parker came next followed by Gail and Dad Shirley. Then two names that meant nothing to Dash.

"Cai Mak?" Dash asked Mickey and Petrusiak when she brought the list to them.

"Doesn't mean anything to me," Mickey said.

"I'll run a check on him," Dash said. "What about this last name—Jean Whitlock?"

Mickey stared at her.

50

When Jean got back to the house, the kitchen had been cleaned, dishes washed, the four women gathered in front of the flat screen television engrossed in *The Bachelor*. Otis, off his leash, happily joined them, snuggling on the sofa.

"This guy, he's a pussy," Zindzi was saying, shaking her head at the handsome *Bachelor* dude with perfect white teeth.

"The women are whores," Deeksha pronounced.

"*We* are the whores," Zindzi countered. "*They* are television stars."

"Whores," confirmed Deeksha.

Polina gasped with pleasure as Jean handed her the cigarettes. "You are goddess," she announced, tearing away at the pack, dashing out of the room, headed Jean imagined, for the backyard.

She was in the kitchen hanging up Otis's leash when her cellphone sounded. Mickey Dann this time. Did anyone other than cops ever phone her? Apparently not.

"What have I done wrong now?" she asked.

"Who says you have done anything wrong?"

"Why else do you call me, other than to give me shit?"

"Come on," he said, "I don't *always* give you shit when I call."

"If it's not shit, why are you calling?"

"Maybe I just want to see you," he said.

"Be still my beating heart," she said.

"I'm serious. Can I come around?"

She glanced at the women in the other room engrossed in their television show. "When?"

"How about right now?"

"Tell you what, I'm going to walk the dog later." A bit of a white lie, since she had just finished Otis's walk.

"That dog doesn't like me."

"Can you blame him?"

"All right," Mickey said. "Where?"

"How about the Cenotaph at eleven?"

"See you then," Mickey said.

Like old times, she thought. Nothing new with Mickey Dann.

Same old same old.

———

The park in front of Milton's old City Hall was deserted except for Mickey waiting on the park bench where she used to meet her late Uncle Jock, Milton's long-serving mayor. Those were fun times for a little girl with her uncle. When she grew into adulthood and Jock began to reveal his true duplicitous colors, the fun times were over.

But Jock was gone, replaced on the park bench by Detective Mickey Dann and she was not certain Mickey was an improvement. Certainly, Otis didn't think so. He bared his teeth as Jean approached the bench.

"Maybe it's not that Otis dislikes me," Mickey said. "It's just that he's nervous and protective when it's dark."

"No," Jean said, sitting beside him. "He doesn't like you."

"A dog reflects his mistress's sensibility I've heard."

"You think I don't like you?"

"I'm never sure."

"Let's see how this meeting goes, and I'll let you know," Jean said.

"We raided a house in Toronto looking for a woman named Shanifa Mahaba. Does that name mean anything to you?"

Jean thought of the Shanifa who tried to shoot her at the motel. She said, "Should it?"

Mickey eyed her suspiciously before continuing. "I believe and so do Toronto detectives that Shanifa, who is probably a victim of sex trafficking herself, is operating a prostitution ring. She also seems to be out for revenge."

"What kind of revenge?"

"The kind of revenge that gets people dead, including the Shirleys. We found a list of the people we think she's going after." Mickey paused for effect. "You're one of the names on that list."

"I see," was all Jean could think to say.

"Other than to observe your lack of surprise, I have a question."

"No surprise there," Jean said.

"Why? Why would you be on the hit list of a homicidal sex trade worker?"

"Supposing I said I have no idea."

"You would be lying."

"Nothing could be further from the truth," Jean said.

"Seriously, Jean. What's going on?"

Jean bought some time, bending down to give Otis, at her feet, a quick pet.

Mickey wasn't buying the attempt at delay: "Jean…"

"Okay, the reason Shanifa wants me dead—and she's already tried once—is because she thinks I'm one of them."

"One of what?"

"She may have concluded that I was hired by the Shirleys to help run their operation. Now that they're dead, Shanifa may think I'm part of a sex ring operated by a pimp named Cai Mak."

"Why the hell would she think that?"

"Because that's what I want everyone to think."

Mickey gave her a stunned look. "What are you doing?"

"Doyle Parker was a CI for the Mounties. They didn't think he was getting them the information they need so they came to me."

"That prick Walter Duke?"

"That's the prick," Jean agreed.

"He told us he had inserted a CI into the Shirleys' operation, but I had no idea it was you."

"It was me," Jean affirmed.

Mickey was shaking his head. "I don't believe it. Why would you put yourself in jeopardy like this?"

"They want me back on the Force. This is the road back."

"Is that what you want?"

"I don't know."

"But you said yes to this crap."

Jean nodded.

"I don't get it. Why?"

"Maybe because it's worthwhile."

"You're kidding."

"There are four young women barely out of their teens back at my house who would be in a lot of trouble if I hadn't gotten them to safety. I'd say that is worthwhile."

Mickey looked even more incredulous. "You have four sex trade workers living with you?"

"No, I have four scared, lost young women."

"We've issued a BOLO for Shanifa Mahaba and for her partner, Maitland Tompkins," Mickey said. "It's a matter of time before either we arrest them out here in Halton or the Toronto cops get them. In the meantime, you and your house guests should lie low and do your best to stay out of harm's way."

"Is that your best advice?"

"Or get help from Walter Duke and his red coats. After all, he got you into this mess in the first place."

"I've got to be going." Jean stood. Otis immediately sprang to his feet.

"Are you listening to anything I've said?"

"Every word," she said.

Mickey made a dismissive gesture with his hand. He looked suddenly sad and exhausted.

"Are you all right?"

"Don't worry about me," Mickey said. He forced a smile as he rose to face her. "What happened to us?"

"What happened?"

"Yeah," he said. "Something's happened. I'm not sure what."

"What's happened, Mickey, is that nothing's happened."

"I thought something would have." He seemed more distracted than ever.

He touched her arm and then wandered off, caught in pools of street light throwing long shadows across the square.

She wanted to call after him, say something.

But say what?

51

The cabin in the woods was not far from the Halton Rock Quarry.

There was a fair amount of toing and froing along winding country roads before Shanifa got her bearings and the van wheeled onto the track leading to a clearing above the quarry.

The cabin stood at the clearing's edge, surrounded by trees, rustic in a traditional-Ontario-cottage kind of way. Shanifa retrieved the key from beneath the stone near the entrance, exactly where she had seen Dad hide it.

"Dad's not-so-secret secret," Shanifa explained as she led Maitland inside. Amber, Nataliya, Daria, Kiva and Bora followed.

"A secret that is no secret?" questioned Amber. "That's no secret."

"No one knew about it except maybe Dad's wife," Shanifa explained. "His wife and the women he brought here and raped."

"But you know about it," Maitland said.

"Yes," Shanifa said. "I know too well." She brightened. "But now the devil is gone and we can put his secret to use."

They brought in the groceries they had acquired on the way out of Toronto, and as best they could made themselves at home in the waning late afternoon light.

Yes, this was good, Shanifa thought, this would do for what she had in mind. She went outside to insert a fresh clip into the Beretta, making certain it was operating properly so there would be no mistakes this time. No more betrayals. Maitland came out of the cabin, watching her.

Well, Shanifa corrected herself, one final betrayal. She stuck the gun in the waistband of her jeans and approached Maitland. "We need to talk."

Maitland blinked a couple of times and said, "Sure."

"Away from the ears of the others."

Maitland nodded uncertainly and then followed Shanifa along a trail that led through the woods up to the edge of the cliff and the water-filled pit glistening under what was left of the afternoon sun.

Shanifa came to a stop and turned to face Maitland. "Dad told me that this place is called the Hidden Quarry. He said he worked it for many years before it played out. When it did, he opened a second quarry, Halton Rock, but he said it was never the same. That's why he became a sex trafficker. That is what he told me."

"It's spectacular," Maitland said. "But what's the point?"

"When Dad brought me here, he drank a lot, and after he finished with me, he always felt remorse and said that it was his wife who made him get into the business, and that he worked for this terrible man and he wished he could get out, but he was trapped."

"But you didn't believe him," Maitland said.

"Of course not," Shanifa said. "Except for the times when he talked about the evil man he worked for."

Maitland's face reflected the confusion she felt. "I don't understand what you're getting at," she said.

"I want you to call him," Shanifa said.

The confusion deepened. "What?"

"Call him. Call Cai Mak. Tell him where we are."

"Are you out of your mind? How could I do that even if I wanted to?"

"You told me you worked alone. That is a lie. You work for him. Or you worked for him. You said it yourself. He was your mentor."

Shanifa pulled out the Beretta. "Call him."

Maitland's confused expression was replaced by alarm. "Shanifa, I don't know what you're talking about. This is all wrong."

"I'm sure he's expecting your call so make it."

"Don't do this, please." The alarm was gone; now there was desperation.

Shanifa took a step forward, the Beretta raised. Between gritted teeth she said, "You have a phone. Call. Tell him where we are."

Tears streamed down Maitland's face. "Please," she said, begging now. "Please...please..."

"Do it," Shanifa said coldly.

———

The women gathered in the cabin's main room were startled when they heard the single gunshot. Amber said she wasn't certain it was a gunshot. But the others had heard enough gunfire in their short lives; they *knew*.

And then there was no more debate after they saw the gun in Shanifa's hand as she re-entered. Everyone grew anxious. No one spoke until Shanifa said, "Maitland is not coming back. Gather your things and leave. It is not safe for you here. The sooner you go, the better. Take the van. I have left a bag for you in the back. There is close to one hundred thousand dollars, courtesy of a very rich man. It is enough to sustain you while you decide what to do with your lives."

Explosions of surprise followed, and then angry questions and demands to know what had happened to Maitland, a cacophony of noise that Shanifa silenced with a wave of her gun. "Enough," she snapped.

"There is nothing left to say. It is finished. Leave. Get out."

There was more confusion, exclamations, demands to know what Shanifa planned to do, and then, finally, acquiescence.

The women loaded themselves into the van. No one spoke. There were no more questions. Only Amber, the comparatively innocent American, allowed a tear. The others were used to hardship, to the unexpected. No hardship here, at least not for the moment, simply the unexpected. The unexpected could be dealt with. If there was danger, and Shanifa said there was, then better not to ask more questions, just get away.

When the van was gone, Shanifa exhaled and went back into the cabin. She sat on the sofa, waiting until she could no longer hear the van on the roadway. For the first time in a long time, she experienced total silence.

She sat back, staring at the gun she held. She began to cry. Where did this come from? she wondered through her tears.

She bent forward, dropping the gun, burying her face in her hands.

Weeping.

Outside, it had become dark.

52

Jean's cellphone began making noises as she came up the walk with Otis. At first, she thought it was Mickey calling to apologize, to tell her he understood what she was doing, admired her for her courage, was sorry and wanted to make it up to her.

But the voice on the other end of the phone wasn't Mickey. "Where are you?"

The elusive Cai Mak, coming up for air.

"It's late," she said.

"I know where Shanifa is hiding. I need you with me."

"You don't need me," Jean said.

"She's tried to kill us both. I was wearing a protective vest. That saved me. She was careless and out of bullets. That saved you. Nothing will stop her from trying again—unless we stop her first."

"Where is she?"

"Not far from the Shirleys' quarry business."

"Near Georgetown."

"That's right."

"How can you be sure?"

"Someone inside works for me. Tell me where you are and I will pick you up."

"No way. I'll meet you," Jean amended.

Cai remained silent for a moment. Then: "Where?"

"There's a traffic light at Acton, north of Milton. I'll be waiting there."

The line went dead.

Jean parked a few yards north of the only stoplight on Acton's deserted Main Street.

As she waited, she was on her cell, once again trying Walter Duke and once again getting his answering machine. She left him a long message and then turned off her phone. That's all she needed, Duke calling while she was with Cai Mak.

She was beginning to worry that he wouldn't show when a black Cadillac Escalade pulled up beside her. Cai Mak was in the passenger seat. One of his shaved-head goons was behind the wheel; another sat in the back. Cai lowered his window. The streetlight glinted off his glasses. "Get in," he ordered.

"I'll follow you," Jean said.

"Do as I say; get in the back."

"Better I follow you."

Cai twisted around and nodded to the shaved-head guy in the rear. He got out and came over to Jean. "The man wants you with us," he said in a tight voice. "Get out and I'll park your car."

At this rate, they would be here all night, Jean thought. She got out and walked to the Cadillac. The air inside the vehicle was full of the smell of men too close together. No one spoke. She stared at the back of

Cai's head until the shaved-head guy came back from parking her car and got in beside her.

"Give me my keys," Jean said.

The shaved-head guy grunted but didn't move.

"Give her the keys." Cai Mak said.

"Sure, no problem," the shaved-head guy said. He tossed Jean the keys. The catch gave her a kind of relief. She could match these clowns. Or, at least, she could catch the keys they threw at her.

53

Shanifa dozed, luxuriating in the silence, the sense of comfort she had not experienced since—well, if she thought about it, she had spent a life without comfort, never quite certain she would be alive or dead.

Or, worst of all, raped.

Repeatedly raped growing up in Malinda, a resort town in Kenya on the Indian Ocean where the tourists arrived in droves each season to rent private villas and be serviced by the pimps who provided young girls like Shanifa. When she was eighteen, the gang she worked for transported her and others to Dubai and the Arab Emirates. There were times when she thought the life there, the unending sexual demands, would kill her; occasionally she thought of taking her own life, but then dismissed the idea. The wicked men who used her would kill her soon enough, she needn't bother.

But she managed to survive. She was tougher than the rest, she told herself; she would make it.

Then she found herself in Toronto, a sex ring run by Cai Mak. He soon moved her west of the city to a satellite operation managed by Gail and Dad Shirley. By now the anger was embedded deep; the red-hot desire to lash out, vengeance for the abuse she had suffered at home and then in Dubai and most recently at the hands of Dad Shirley.

What upset her most was the constant noise: shouted orders, angry demands. Never a moment of peace, time to herself. Until this evening. Finally, totally, alone. The beautiful silence. Not for long, she thought sadly. Soon enough the silence would end; the noise would return.

But for now...

She stood, picking up the Beretta. She racked the slide to insert a shell into the chamber so that it was ready to fire. She reached around and tucked the gun into the waistband at the small of her back.

Shanifa took a final look around. You could clean up this place and have a very nice life here, she thought.

A life she would never have.

Drawing a deep breath, she opened the front door and went out.

———————

The moon above the quarry shone against a black night.

Jean gave an involuntary shiver as the Cadillac came to a stop. The shaved-head guy behind the wheel turned off the engine and everyone sat in silence. Then Cai announced, "Let's get this over with," and ejected himself from the front seat.

Jean got out, stretching her legs. The shaved-head guys now had guns in their hands. So did Cai, examining Jean as though attempting to come to a decision about her authenticity.

Then, as though deciding conclusions were impossible, he turned away, starting through the buckthorn trees that pressed against this side of the quarry. A sweeping wind shook their spindly branches, producing a sound like a death rattle, transforming the woods into a foreboding Haunted Forest out of *The Wizard of Oz* with Jean cast as Dorothy, following Cai, accompanied by the two shaved-head guys.

They broke out of the trees, the wind whistling hard against them, and abruptly the quarry was directly ahead. Far below Jean could see the outlines of big trucks and huge earth-moving machines, prehistoric iron monsters at rest, with the Shirleys gone perhaps never to start again.

Cai Mak turned to Jean and said, "This is as far as you go."

Jean looked at him, her stomach dropping. "What are you talking about?"

The shaved-head guys sprang forward, taking Jean's arms. Big guys, she thought fleetingly, muscles like rocks. Somewhere in the distance she heard the voice of Cai Mak saying, "It's tricky in the darkness."

He nodded at the two men. They began dragging Jean forward. She struggled, but she might as well have been fighting two stone slabs. The edge of the cliff was outlined in moonlight and then a black void the moon could not reach. Jean heard herself scream, eyes involuntarily closing.

The gunshot, followed immediately by a spray of warm blood splashing her face, and one of the slabs was gone. The other let go of Jean so he could fumble for his gun. Jean found herself on the ground. Two more shots and he jerked away, dropping the gun.

From her vantage point down on all fours, Jean saw Cai Mak wheel, gun raised at a distracted Shanifa. Jean grabbed the nearby gun and fired in Cai's direction. The bullet struck his shoulder and jerked him around. He was still on his feet, trying to get a shot off. Jean fired again and the bullet struck him smack in the forehead. He fell back and in a flash was gone, disappearing over the cliff, devoured by the darkness.

That left Shanifa and Jean, both with guns, eyes fixed on each other, the wind howling around them.

"I should kill you," Shanifa said.

"No, no you shouldn't. I'm not your enemy."

"Everyone is my enemy."

"All your enemies are gone," Jean said. "Mine too. There's only us now. We shouldn't harm each other."

Shanifa considered this. Her every instinct told her to pull the trigger. Pulling the trigger ended this with certainty. Otherwise, there was more uncertainty and she didn't want that. Couldn't deal with that.

She would have fired, but the sudden overhead clatter stopped her. She glanced up to see the helicopter lowering toward them; a powerful searchlight bathed them in a drizzle of dazzling white, the noise growing even louder, so that she could hardly hear the howl of the oncoming police sirens.

Noise, always noise. She must go where there is quiet, where she could finally find the tranquility that had always eluded her.

She dropped her arm and released the Beretta from her grasp.

Jean saw the gun drop to the ground. Shanifa was a shadow against the whiteness of the light, an ethereal creature, shoulders back, head high, walking forward. It took a moment for Jean to realize what Shanifa was about to do. She cried out, "No!" And started running.

Shanifa reached the edge of the quarry. The moon above, the pitch blackness below.

The welcoming blackness.

Jean cried out again, reaching for her. Shanifa turned and Jean had a glimpse of the smile on her face and then she was gone. No sound. Nothing.

Just gone.

54

The RCMP confirmed that Polina, Zindzi, Deeksha, and Maitha were in fact victims of the international sex trafficking trade, and so the four were granted temporary residence visas by Canadian immigration authorities. The five women who had been working for Shanifa and Maitland were arrested near Montreal. Immigration was in the process of ascertaining their status.

Jean knew the future of her house guests remained in doubt, but for now there was the excitement of starting anew—excitement mixed with trepidation and tears. Not to mention a promise or two. "I stop smoking for you, Jean," Polina announced. "I swear to you I will stop."

Jean cast a skeptical look—"I know you'll do your best, Polina,"—and then hugged her. The others embraced Jean and there were more tears before they piled into the van that would take them into Toronto.

Inspector Walter Duke pulled into her drive almost as soon as the van departed. It was as if he had been waiting for the women to leave before making an appearance. Jean crossed her arms—a defensive gesture? she wondered—as he got out of his car, dressed in standard gray business-suit mufti and lumbered across to where she waited.

"Tearful farewells?" he asked.

"Not me," Jean said, only too aware of the wetness of her cheeks. "I'm far too tough."

"I can see that." Duke delivered his version of a smile. "You know what I'd love right now? I'd love a cup of coffee."

"Come inside," Jean said.

He followed her into the kitchen. Otis stretched out on his day bed, immediately sat up, spotting Duke and making a low growling sound.

"Is he friendly?" Duke asked.

"Apparently, he doesn't like cops," Jean said.

"I'm sorry to hear that," Duke said with a thin smile.

"Why don't you go into the living room. I'll bring the coffee. How do you take it?"

"Black," Duke said.

"I should have known," Jean said.

"What?" Duke looked slightly amused. "Mounties always drink their coffee black?"

"And they always get their man," Jean replied dryly.

Otis followed Duke out of the kitchen. When Jean came in with the coffee a few minutes later, Otis was on his haunches, facing Duke, in case the inspector turned out to be the trouble Otis suspected he was.

"Everyone is impressed with the job you've done," Duke said after taking a sip of his coffee.

"I avoided getting myself killed, not much more than that," Jean said.

"Bringing down the Toronto base of an international sex trade ring, I'd say that was quite an accomplishment," Duke said.

"Shanifa Mahaba had a lot more to do with that," Jean said.

"Yes, but her methods left a lot to be desired."

"Still, she pretty much got the job done," Jean said. "Did you know she was from Kenya?"

"I understand that was the case," Duke said.

"Mahaba. It's Swahili for love. Something I don't believe she ever found."

"I know this has taken a toll on you," Duke began.

"I keep seeing her, in that moment before she leapt. The smile on her face. The peacefulness of it. Who knows what she had gone through in her life to arrive at the edge of that cliff."

"Yes," Duke said.

"She haunts me," Jean said.

Duke did not know how to respond. They sat in silence. Otis stretched on the floor.

"I'd like you to come back," Duke said finally.

"That's what you've said."

"To us. To the Force."

"I don't know," Jean said.

"I think you do, Jean. There are people who when faced with danger run away from it. Then there are the few who run toward the danger. You are one of those rare people who runs toward it."

"There are those who might think I'm crazy for doing that," Jean said.

"Those people are not part of the Force," Duke said. "The Force is full of people like you, Jean."

"That may be a sign of madness, not an indication I should join a police force."

"Think about it." Duke got to his feet.

She walked him to the door. "Doyle Parker."

"What about him?" Duke asked.

"I hear he's out of the hospital."

"Charged with everything but jaywalking."

"Then he's in custody?"

Duke just looked at her.

"Don't tell me he's out."

"He's more useful to us out of jail than he is in," Duke said.

"You're kidding."

"He's been warned to keep his nose clean." Duke didn't sound very convincing.

"Bullshit. The Doyle Parkers of the world don't keep their noses clean."

"It'll be fine," Duke said.

"No, it won't," Jean said.

———

The deep-blue late-summer sky filled with dramatic cloud shapes, throwing shifting shadows across open fields yet undisturbed by developers.

As Jean drove into Georgetown, she saw that Main Street South was blocked off for the weekly Farmers' Market.

She detoured through side streets until she reached Mill Street and parked. Mothers pushed baby carriages, grandparents marched with sun-hatted grandchildren, gaggles of teenage girls in jean shorts waving cellphones talked excitedly together, everyone off to the market.

Jean climbed the steps to the porch of the white-frame house with the hanging flower pots and knocked on the screen door. For a couple of minutes there was no response. A second knock brought movement on the other side of the screen. A surprised Daye wore jeans, a short-sleeved white blouse and a nervous expression. "Jean," she said in a slightly breathless voice.

"Hi, Daye. I was in the neighborhood and thought I'd drop by and see how you're doing."

"In the neighborhood?" There was suspicion in her voice.

"Can I come in?"

Daye opened the screen door and stepped out on the porch. "I'm glad to see you, Jean. But now is not a good time."

"I'm sorry," Jean said. "I didn't mean to intrude."

"No, it's all right. You're not intruding—"

From inside the house, a voice called, "Daye, what's happening?"

A pale and thin Doyle Parker opened the screen door. His arm was in a cast. He was unshaven and bleary-eyed and not happy to see Jean. "What the hell," he said.

"It's all right, Doyle," Daye said in a high voice. "Let me handle this."

"What's this bitch doing here?"

"Doyle. You promised," Daye said in a commanding tone.

"Jesus Christ." Doyle slammed the screen door shut and disappeared from view. Jean could hear him inside, swearing loudly. She faced Daye. "I need to talk to you."

Jean came down off the porch onto the sidewalk. Daye followed, nervously rubbing at her forearm. "I know what it looks like," Daye said.

"Looks like you and Doyle are back together," Jean said.

Daye frowned and said, "We've had long talks. Doyle's changed. All this crap that's gone down, he's had, I guess, an epiphany. He's not the same man he was before."

"Daye, he's been charged with sex trafficking. He's going to jail."

"He's pleaded innocent to the charges." The words came out of her mouth but there was no confidence in them.

"He's guilty. He's going away for a long time."

"All the more reason why, right now, he needs someone to stand by him. To provide support."

"What about your friend Peter?"

"Peter is no longer in the picture," Daye said.

"What happened?"

"He decided to break it off."

"Because you're seeing Doyle?"

"I don't know," Daye said. "He's back with his wife. So, there you go."

"I don't believe this," Jean said.

"I don't expect you to understand. But I understand. That's what counts. I understand and I love him."

Jean's gaze met Daye's. She fumbled for something to say, words that would convince her cousin. All she could think of was, "This is a huge mistake."

Daye's mouth tightened. "It's good to see you, Jean."

She turned and strode back up to the porch and into the house. The screen door banged shut.

Jean stood on the sidewalk feeling numb. Then she walked back to her car and got in. On the way out of Georgetown, the big clouds turned black, obscuring the sun.

It looked as though it was going to rain.

55

Inspector Walter Duke called often. Jean ignored his calls. She didn't want to talk to anyone, certainly not anyone anxious to discuss her future. What future? For now, she wanted only the daily routine of walking Otis, aimless attempts at taking care of her garden, reading a Margaret Atwood novel, binge watching *Big Little Lies*—a subject she knew a great deal about.

Not thinking failed. In the quiet moments she so longed for, Jean's mind swirled with thoughts of everything. The running helped. After the walks with Otis she would put on her sweats and pound around the Mill Pond, trying to outrun the demons that kept invading her head. Sometimes it worked.

This bright summer morning the endorphins kicked in the way they were supposed to. Overwhelmed with an unexpected feeling of well-being, she decided to reward herself with a latte.

At this time of the day, the interior of the Main Street Starbucks wasn't busy. She ordered the latte, resisted temptation offered by a blueberry scone. A voice behind her said, "I got a new truck."

She swung around to the handsome, unshaven face of Jim Callahan. "Remember me?" he asked. "The guy from the quarry?"

"What kind of truck did you get?" she asked.

"You do remember." He actually looked relieved.

"You bought me coffee. How could I forget?"

"I'm just about to get another coffee. Have you got time to join me?"

"I guess so, sure."

"Do you want anything? Something to eat?"

"Thanks. I'm resisting the scones."

"A disciplined woman, I like that," he said.

"Only when it comes to scones," Jean said.

Jim went to the counter to order his coffee while Jean found a seat at a corner table, feeling—what *was* she feeling?—well, sort of pleased that she had encountered this guy again. Ordering herself not to overthink this as Jim joined her with his coffee and a slice of banana bread.

"I feel guilty about it," he said.

"You should never feel guilty about banana bread," Jean said.

"You want some?"

"No, then I'll start to feel guilty."

"Even though you shouldn't feel guilty about banana bread," Jim said.

"Correct."

He took a bite, accompanied by a look of satisfaction. "A GMC Sierra."

"What?"

"You asked me what kind of truck I bought."

"Okay. The GMC Sierra. Is that a good thing?"

"It's designed and built to get things done," he said.

"Glad to hear it."

"I bought it to impress you."

"You bought a truck to impress me?"

"The fact that the old one broke down and wouldn't start also helped," Jim said.

"Did you drive to Milton to show off your new truck?"

"Could be." Jim took the time to swallow before he added, "Then again, I had some business in town. On my way out, I decided to get a coffee and lo and behold, here you are."

"Dripping sweat, unfortunately. You never seem to catch me at my best."

"I don't know about that," Jim said, smiling.

"Well, however you got here, it's good to see you," Jean said.

"I was wondering if I might run into you," Jim said. "I almost called again, but from what I can understand, you've been pretty busy."

Jean made a face. "You've been reading the newspapers."

"Television these days," Jim said. "Are you all right?"

"That depends on your definition of 'all right,'" Jean said.

"The definition that means you've come through."

"In that case, yes, I've come through," Jean said. "Not sure how well, but I'm still standing."

"I've thought a lot about that day at the quarry," Jim said.

"Have you?"

"What you must have been experiencing. Here I thought you were an attractive hiker willing to have coffee with a stranger."

"That's me all right." She smiled when she said it.

"I had no idea you were a Mountie."

"Ex-Mountie," Jean said.

"A cop," Jim said. He smiled when he said it.

"Is that a problem?"

"Not at all. In fact, I find it kind of intriguing."

Three quarters of an hour later, Jean walked with Jim back to where a big red truck was parked. "This is the truck?"

"The GMC Sierra. You like it?"

"It's a...red truck," she said.

"Very astute," he said. "I'd like to see you again."

"I should have been more enthusiastic about the truck," she said.

"Never mind. I'd still like to see you."

"Yes, I'd like that, too," she said.

"I'm supposed to do what we call a trail break next weekend outside Georgetown. Nothing too arduous. There's the Georgetown market Saturday morning. Have you been to it?"

"Not to the market," Jean said.

"We could meet, have a coffee, wander around the market a bit and then do the hike. How does that sound?"

"Sounds like fun," Jean said.

"Then let's do it."

She nodded and then neither of them said anything for a time, keeping their eyes on one another. She reached up and kissed him on the mouth.

"Next Saturday," she said.

56

The Georgetown Market in a blur on a perfect Saturday morning, Main Street packed beneath a blue sky, Jean safe and comfortable, enjoying the closeness of this man Jim Callahan as together they inspected the stalls lining the street, bakery offerings here, flaky samosas there, lattes from a local café, ease and laughter.

Bliss.

Well, as close to bliss as Jean's automatically triggered defensive mechanisms would allow; the cop's fundamental hesitation to take things, no matter how seemingly good, at face value. The mechanisms broke down further following lunch—she forgave him the so-so Italian restaurant, the world overwhelmed with so-so Italian restaurants.

Their post-lunch destination, Jim announced, was the Hungry Hollow Trail a few miles outside Georgetown. Not so much a hike, Jean was relieved to discover, as a stroll on a boardwalk dappled in sunlight through woods, past marshes and ponds with a pause on a bridge over a silver stream that allowed Jim to lean on the railing next to Jean and quite naturally—it certainly *felt* natural—reach over and kiss her. Allowing him to take her in his arms seemed the perfectly natural extension of that kiss and led to more intense kissing, Jean, fleetingly thinking that this was crazy but then crazy on a Saturday afternoon seemed perfectly fine.

She could not recall any discussion about it, but after they finished with the trail or as much of it as they wanted to navigate before losing interest in the face of their need to be with each other, they ended up at his elegant two-story house on Georgetown's outskirts.

Unexpected, she thought as she nursed a glass of chardonnay on the enclosed veranda overlooking a garden much healthier-looking than anything in her backyard. Truck-driving, baseball cap-wearing, casually dressed, outdoorsy, environmentally conscious, sort-of-rugged-looking, all those adjectives applied to Jim and perhaps a few more, but nothing about him that would have inspired thoughts of elegance.

But then there was this, well, *elegant* house.

"Deep in thought?" Jim at the threshold, coming from the kitchen.

"Thinking what a lovely house," she answered.

"For a guy who wanders through the woods and drives a truck," Jim said.

"And fights for a better world," she said, laughing.

"Well, at least a world with fewer quarries in it." He leaned down to kiss her.

So natural, she thought. And fun. Fun kissing Jim Callahan. She kissed him some more.

As it grew dark, they dined in the backyard on the thin-sliced strip loin Jim barbecued on a grill after first marinating it. The steak would not have been her first choice, at least not at this health-conscious time of her life, but she had to admit it was delicious.

Pleased, he poured more wine, a rich merlot, not her color of choice but pleasant, nonetheless. By the time they finished, the night had closed in with stars making an appearance in case atmospheric additions were needed.

Jean finished the merlot, feeling the warming effects of the wine, igniting an emotion she had not felt for a long time: desire.

She rose and went around the table, leaned down, positioning her hands on either side of his face to kiss him deeply. A voice said, "Let's go inside."

Was that her voice? Yes, good God, it was.

Jim took her hand and led her into the house. There was a blur of living room and hallway, a staircase, a door opening, the darkness of a master bedroom, the deep rasp of desire, Jean wondering where the sound came from before realizing it was coming from her as he undressed her.

On a king-size bed, his hand between her legs as she held what she announced was an impressively big cock. There was no time for further discussions of size or anything else because he was sliding all-too-easily inside her, both of them awfully noisy about it.

Finally, they rested. Jean's breathing regaining some normalcy, her heart stopped feeling as though it would explode out her chest. He wrapped her in his arms, murmured something she didn't quite catch.

And then he began again.

God, she thought. So soon? But if he was ready then so was she. More than ready, she discovered. Ravenous. Making up for lost time. A *lot* of lost time, swiftly climaxing, and then climaxing again and again.

That cock, she thought; her last thought before drifting into a deep sleep.

———————

Jean came awake slowly, inhaling the smell of—*no*, couldn't be—eggs and bacon? She sat up, alone in the big bed in his bedroom. This guy could not be downstairs preparing a Sunday morning breakfast of bacon and eggs.

Could he?

I mean, Jean thought, this guy couldn't be *that* nice. It was too much of a good thing.

Wasn't it?

She smiled to herself as she got out of bed. No, she decided, after what she had experienced the last few years there could not be too much of a good thing. There could only be a good thing.

The splash of sunshine through the big windows at the side of the room triggered the headache that reminded her she'd drunk too much red wine the night before, the red wine she would never otherwise have consumed had she not been on her way to getting laid.

And she had gotten *laid* she concluded as she padded naked across the impressive sisal carpeting into a marbled bathroom with a walk-in shower the size of a closet. A guy with a great bathroom, rare to say the least. If she remembered correctly, Mickey Dann didn't

have a remarkable bathroom. Mickey didn't have a remarkable anything.

Bending over the sink, she splashed cold water
on her face. That revived her somewhat. She looked
around, trying to decide whether to take a shower. Was
that too much? A one-night stand—was that what it
was?—and then you take a shower in the guy's house?
What was single-night sex etiquette here? Was a shower acceptable under these circumstances? She was way
out of the loop when it came to morning-after proto-
col. Right now, though, she needed a towel to dry her
face. The towel racks were empty.

Back in the bedroom, Jean spied a walk-in closet. The mirrored sliding door was open. She entered.
There was not much in the way of clothing on the
racks, but on the shelves above, she could see a pile
of neatly folded towels. She reached up, unexpectedly
dislodging a porcelain-blue leather jewelry box.

The jewelry box hit the floor, spilling its contents—
rings, women's watches, necklaces, bracelets.

And an earring.

A silver earring with distinctive silver tassels.

The nude body floated in front of her, drifting up
from a submerged van at the bottom of her consciousness. The nude body of a young woman.

Floating through the murk. Jean could reach out
and touch that body.

That nude body. A silver-tasseled earring.

Caught in Jean's consciousness. Seared onto her
brain.

57

Jean knelt on the closet floor holding the earring. Rising to her feet, she stepped into the bedroom as the door opened and Jim Callahan, still nude, carried in a tray containing two cups of coffee and toast. He stopped, the smile dropping from his face as he saw the earring Jean held. For a moment, neither of them said anything. Then he casually said, "I'm going to need that back."

Jean lashed out with her foot, kicking the tray out of his hands. The cups along with the tray went flying, hot coffee spraying across Jim's face and chest. He cried out, reeling, allowing Jean to knock him aside so that she could dash past him into the corridor. The stairs loomed ahead. Behind her, Jim was calling her name.

Jean bolted down the stairs, taking two steps at a time. She was nearly at the bottom when suddenly Jim was right behind her, coming close enough so that he could get off a kick that caught her on her leg. She spilled forward, all her weight coming down on her right foot, producing a white-hot knife blade of pain. She hit the floor, Jim slamming down on top of her, knocking the wind out of her.

"Jean," he breathed into her ear. "Stop this. We need to talk."

But there was no talk, just his rough, hard hands tightening around her throat, her rising terror as he began to cut off her windpipe. Dimly, she realized that somehow, she still had the silver earring gripped in her hand.

Jim twisted her slowly around to get a better grip. She looked up into his face, drained of its handsomeness his eyes black and emotionless with the effort to kill her. She jabbed the earring, tassels gleaming, into that black eye, deep into the socket.

Blood sprayed as he issued a high-pitched scream, loosening his grip on her throat. She struggled to her feet as Jim writhed on the floor holding his bloody eye.

She lurched into the kitchen with him suddenly resurrected and right behind her, ignoring the blood spurting from his eye, slamming her against the stove. The cast-iron skillet on a front burner, the bacon bubbling and spitting in hot grease, Jim's quick hands at her throat, once again choking her.

Jean's grasping fingers brushed the pan handle. Her free hand clutched his groin, taking that long tumescent thing in her hand, twisting hard.

He cried out and the hands no longer choked her. She lifted the skillet, hot grease and bacon splashing his naked chest and face. He was screaming louder, falling back, holding his head.

She moved away from the stove, holding the skillet, using it as a weapon to strike him. Jim went down on the floor.

She had a moment raising the skillet when she thought she might kill him. Kill the deceitful, murdering bastard.

Kill him good.

But she got hold of herself, dropping the skillet. She looked around, saw the earring lying in pool of blood. She limped over and picked it up.

On the floor, Jim Callahan twitched and made a sound that was part whimper, part groan. Jean hovered over him.

"I don't even like bacon," she said.

58

It's badly sprained but not broken," the youthful emergency room doctor explained as she showed Jean two X-ray photographs of her foot. The doctor was Asian, black hair pulled back into a bun, glasses with dark frames that emphasized her efficiency.

"Also," the young doctor continued, "the CT scan shows you've got two cracked ribs. A few other bruises and contusions. But otherwise, you seem to be okay. They used to employ compression wraps for the ribs, but not any longer because they prevent you from deep breathing and that can lead to pneumonia."

"Then what do I do?" asked Jean.

"Lots of icing on the foot and ribs," the young doctor said. "That and rest."

The door opened and Mickey Dann leaned in. "Okay, if I come in?"

The young doctor nodded. "We're finished here. The patient can go home."

Jean thanked her, the young doctor smiled professionally and slipped away, leaving Jean with Mickey.

"No more questions," Jean declared in a tired voice. "I'm all questioned out."

"Just wanted to make sure you're all right," Mickey said.

"Liar. You want to know what I was doing with Jim Callahan."

"Hey, it's your life," Mickey said.

She shot him a disbelieving look. "Yeah, right. Some life."

"There is one thing," Mickey said.

"Aha. You're not here because you're concerned about my well-being."

"Of course, I'm concerned."

"But?"

"Callahan is here."

"What do you mean 'here?'"

"Down the hall."

"How is he?"

"Not great, thanks to you, but he is able to talk."

"Good."

"The only person he's willing to talk to is you."

"I don't want to talk to him," Jean said.

"But you do want to find out what happened to those three women."

Jean looked at him. He met her gaze with raised eyebrows.

"Shit," she said.

Mickey drew a mini recorder device from his pocket and handed it to her. "Use this," he said.

———

Two uniformed officers stood guard outside Jim Callahan's hospital room. One of the officers nodded at Jean, then pushed open the door so that she could enter into the semi-darkness of the room. A curtain was pulled around the bed in which Callahan lay on his back, his head wrapped in bandages. A bandage covered his right eye. The Invisible Man, Jean thought as she stood at the bottom of the bed. She took note of the oxygen attached to him as well as IV lines feeding him antibiotics. Nearby, a portable heater and humidifier made soft humming sounds.

Jim's mouth opened and closed as though the attempt to produce words was too much for him. Finally, he mumbled, "You...almost killed me."

"I think it was the other way around," Jean said.

"I've...lost an eye..."

"You told the detective you wanted to talk, so talk."

He forced a grin. "Business..."

She pulled up a chair and took out the mini recorder and switched it on, placing it on the tray table beside his bed. "With your permission, I'm going to record this," she said formally.

"Confession," he said.

"How those three women ended up dead in the Hidden Quarry."

"A friend...Not so much a friend. An escort...She introduced me to some of her associates in the sex trade. There was money to be made, they said...bringing young women into the country, grooming them properly and then making them available."

"For sex," Jean added.

"Makes the world go around, doesn't it? Everyone wants it...But it's not always so easy to come by. You hire someone...you get what you pay for...desire fulfilled...No muss. No fuss. The ease of the transaction. That's what makes it appealing."

The more Jim talked, the easier his words seemed to flow. Jim related how he had acquired—his word, *acquired*—three eighteen-year-olds. He insisted he had made certain that was their true age. He did not want to deal with anyone under age. They would stay with him, and he thought that would be great, three beautiful young women available when he wanted them. All he had to do was provide room and board, and make sure they got to the clients—the whales as they were known in the business—arranged through discreet social media ads.

But no sooner had the product been delivered and settled into his house, then there was trouble. The three spoke little English, ate constantly, smoked in his house, demanded drugs, and when they weren't being angry and combative, they broke down in tears of despair. One evening he returned home from a hike and found they had run away.

"The slaves leaving the plantation," Jean observed cynically.

"I didn't look at it that way," Jim said. "I…thought I was being good to them…"

"Pimping them out."

"That's not what I would call it," Jim insisted.

"I wonder what the women called it," Jean said.

The women didn't get far, Jim continued, probably because they had no real idea where they were or where to go. He found the three after dark huddled and scared amid the buckthorn trees adjacent to the Hidden Quarry. He forced them to strip so they couldn't run away again, leaving their clothes in a pile that he planned to retrieve later. One of the women began to scream.

"She became...hysterical," Jim related. "I managed to get her...into the van. The other two...upset, but did as they were told...got in...When I started back along the roadway next to the quarry...they both attacked me. I lost control and it went off the road and into the quarry...I managed to get out." He paused for a time before adding, "The others...didn't."

The act of confession appeared to exhaust him. He lay back, breathing through his mouth. She rose to her feet. He looked at her questioningly. "Enough?"

She shook her head. "What you've told me," Jean said.

"Yes?" His look was expectant.

"It's bullshit."

He shook his head. "No..."

"There was no accident," Jean said. "It was all planned. The van you were driving was stolen. In your basement, detectives found the three women's clothes, along with garments belonging to other women. That jewelry box I found, in addition to the earring, it was full of jewelry, trophies taken from other victims."

"No...other victims," he protested weakly. "It *was* an accident...no plan...not supposed to happen."

"You kidnapped those women, held them captive. From the evidence, it looks as though you've done this before. We'll see. When the women escaped you caught up with them, stripped them naked and then drove them to the quarry. You jumped out of the van a moment before it went into the pit, knowing the three women wouldn't survive, that the van would probably never be found. What you weren't expecting was the bodies of the two women to surface. But then what did it matter, right, Jim? They were nobodies, after all. Play toys who wouldn't play, therefore expendable."

Jim lay silent, except for the harsh sound of his mouth-breathing. Jean swallowed the bile she tasted in her throat. She stood and reached over to click off the recorder. His hand grabbed her wrist. "Got me all wrong...Jean."

"No, I don't."

His grip on her wrist tightened. "We *had* something."

She yanked her arm away and picked up the recorder.

Mickey waited in the corridor as Jean stumbled out of the room. Her gave her a questioning look. She handed him the recorder as she brushed past. He caught up to her along the corridor. "Hey, are you all right?"

"Don't talk to me," she said. "I don't want to talk to anyone."

Jean left Mickey standing there. She didn't allow herself to cry until she reached the parking lot. She couldn't remember where she had parked her goddamn vehicle. Goddamn everything, anyway.

She stood in the lot alone, sobbing.

———

Jean drove home. Otis was happy to see her when she came into her house, demanding pets. She scratched around his ears. He made pleased whimpering sounds. She put the leash on him and then took him for a walk.

A woman and her dog. She wasn't alone. She had Otis. That was enough, she told herself, beginning to feel better.

Acknowledgements

By one count, there are forty quarries in south-western Ontario. The rock used in construction of the highways and roadways we travel on, all the high-rises that have sprung up in urban centers, comes from local quarries.

As commercial and housing development explodes across the region, the quarries have become more and more controversial because of what they can do to everything from the environment to traffic congestion to water quality. Although they are often hidden away behind thick foliage bordering meandering country roads, quarries are very much a sometimes-uneasy fact of southwestern Ontario life.

Walter Heyden was kind enough to provide a quick tour around Ontario's second largest working quarry. I met him thanks to my neighbor, Brad Yundt.

I must stress, if it is even necessary when talking about a work of fiction, that the quarry I visited has nothing to do with anything that happens in the book. It further goes without saying that any mistakes are mine; I take responsibility for them.

Many thanks also to Bill Mungall who I was fortunate to meet through my friend and neighbor, Doug Mohan. Bill describes himself as a lifelong Ontario public servant, now retired, an avid skier, cyclist, backpacker, and canoeist who has led his Guelph-based hiking club on more than two hundred hikes.

Bill not only alerted me to a number of abandoned quarries in the Halton region, but generously gave up an afternoon to show Kathy and me the stunning Dolime Quarry bordering Guelph. Although it's geographically in the wrong place, the Dolime served well as the template for the abandoned quarry portrayed in the book.

Bill also provided a bit of inspiration for one of the characters in the story. I hope he forgives me.

Thanks as well to Debbie Stokes and Juliette Jackson who respectively planted the seeds that grew into *The Hidden Quarry*.

The novel was finished as the global pandemic hit full force and we all found ourselves quarantined. For a writer, this state of affairs is known as Pretty-Much-Business-As-Usual. Still, it helps to have the world's best quarantine partner. My wife, Kathy, makes it fun, conjures fantastic culinary delights, and serves as irreplaceable first reader. And, oh yeah, in her spare time, she came up with the idea for the cover.

Alexandra Lenhoff, as she has for most of the books I've written since the 1990s, once again helpfully read through the manuscript. Longtime friend and novelist, David Kendall, as he always does, saved me from myself countless times. If these books are any good at all, it is due in large part to the forensic eye and studious attention to detail that David brings to bear.

Speaking of a forensic eye, James Bryan Simpson has become a new addition to the editorial team, our closer. As I suspected he would, Bryan found things missed by everyone else.

My lifelong pal, Ray Bennett in London, England, diligently reviewed the galleys. Designer Jennifer Smith once again outdid herself creating and executing the cover.

Finally, my brother, Ric Base, co-ordinates the production of West-End Books from Florida with endless patience and professionalism.

Bro, as I always say, none of this would be possible without you.

A MESSAGE TO READERS

One of the joys of writing these Milton Mystery novels is hearing from readers. So please, don't be shy. Send comments, observations, possible plotlines, philosophical thoughts, even—gulp!—criticism to ron-base@ronbase.com.

Better yet, let others know what you think of these books. Reviews on Amazon.com or Amazon.ca are a great help in alerting other readers to the books. So please don't hesitate to write a review online. Either way, let's keep in touch!

Murder. Mystery. Deception. Deceit.

Ron Base's thrilling Milton Mysteries will keep you up late and turning pages.

THE ESCARPMENT

A young woman's body is discovered at the bottom of the Niagara Escarpment. Did she jump? Or was she pushed? Former Royal Canadian Mounted Police corporal Jean Whitlock has returned in disgrace to Milton, Ontario, the town west of Toronto where she grew up. Jean can't help but be drawn into the mystery surrounding the woman's death. Her future uncertain, her life suddenly in danger, Jean must overcome powerful forces arrayed against her in order to uncover the town's secrets as well as the truth of her own family's dark past. *The Escarpment* is a page-turning thriller from Ron Base, author of the Sanibel Sunset Detective mystery novels. It is the first in a series of Milton Mysteries featuring Jean Whitlock.

THE MILL POND

Disgraced former Royal Canadian Mounted Police Corporal Jean Whitlock has returned to her hometown of Milton, Ontario, to try to put her life back together. It's not working out very well. There is a body in the Mill Pond that Jean knows far too much about. The obsessed Mountie sergeant who tried to rape her in Afghanistan and then left her for dead, has shown up in Milton, once again threatening her life. Before she knows it, Jean is entangled in a dark web of blackmail, murder, local corruption and a far-reaching criminal conspiracy. She must learn all over again that the peaceful small town where she grew up isn't so peaceful anymore. *The Mill Pond* is Ron Base's riveting follow-up to *The Escarpment,* the first Milton Mystery.

MAIN STREET, MILTON

Milton's mayor is found dangling from a lamp-post on Main Street. The mayor's death draws former Royal Canadian Mounted Police corporal Jean Whitlock into a web of lies, deceit—and murder! There is a desperate developer who will stop at nothing to push through his controversial townhouse project. The town's first Sikh mayor discovers rooting out the corruption left behind by his predecessor is not easy. The Ontario premier, known as the Red Queen, worries that her many secrets are in danger of being exposed. A crime lord is dying of cancer, but willing to kill anyone who gets in his way—including Jean Whitlock. *Main Street, Milton* is the third installment in Ron Base's popular Milton Mysteries series

Made in the USA
Middletown, DE
18 May 2020

95143430R00175